Safe at Home

No Ordinary Family Book 2

LINDA BARRETT

DEDICATION

To Mike, my one and only—

We've had some curve balls thrown our way through the years, but never missed an inning.

Thank you for sharing your strength, smarts and heart with me. Thanks for being half of our wonderful team!

Cover art by Shelley Kay at Web Crafters

E-book and print formatting by Web Crafters

www.webcraftersdesign.com

CHAPTER ONE

An organized mess.

Megan Ross stood behind her desk and reviewed the colored folders, calendars, lists and the dozen printouts she'd need for the coming week. She preferred blending manual and electronic methods when creating her schedules. Each worked for her, and to succeed, planning ahead was key. She needed a road map to ensure the public events for the Houston Astro players were a success every time the men interacted with their fans and supporters. If they screwed up, she'd have to make it right with all involved. She'd done that in the past—but, fortunately, mishaps didn't often happen.

A majority of the athletes were professional in all aspects of their career. Including public relations. One or two, however… just overgrown boys. A pair of green eyes came to mind, and her mouth tightened in frustration. Brian Delaney had so much talent but was so undependable on and off the field. She never counted on him showing up for a planned event. He was just a guy riding on good looks and an arm—when he used it. She shook her head at the waste. If she ever stopped to think about what could go wrong in her job, she'd have a meltdown.

Chuckling and dismissing the idea, she sat in front of her computer and began filtering appearance requests. She loved working for the Astros, and she loved her position as Player Promotions and Events Coordinator. Adding to her good fortune was a recent opportunity for promotion to manager. More money, more responsibility. She'd updated her resume and thought she had a good shot. In her competitive world, however, she didn't count on it.

When her desk phone rang, she saw Dave Evans's name on the readout. The team manager. She and Dave had a good rapport, communicated well, but didn't often overlap in their functions. Curious, she picked up the receiver and leaned back in her chair.

"Hey, Megan — come on up to my office for a minute. We've got a little something for you, just up your alley."

"We? Okay, you've got my attention. I'll be right there."

In fact, she'd run. Cooperation and a positive attitude were the keys for a single mom to enjoy job security and support her son.

With a smile on her face and a laptop under her arm, Megan quickly made her way up one flight to the fifth floor of the building, historic Union Station, home of the Astros and Minute Maid Park. She waved to Carla Weston in the outer office and knocked on Dave's doorframe as his door was open. He waved her in.

"Scott and Rick are with us today," said Dave, nodding toward the general manager of the organization and the pitching coach.

"Now you've got me very curious," said Megan, after greeting the men and taking an available chair. She was also a bit concerned. Two of the men directly coached players, while the third reported to the owner of the team. She didn't fit in with this group.

"We're glad you could join us," began Dave.

"Well, of course." She looked from one face to the other. "None of you seem too happy, so..." She gulped, a horrible thought entering her mind. "Am I in some kind of trouble?"

They all spoke at once, but she was attuned to Dave's voice. "Not at all, Megan. In fact, just the opposite. We've got a little situation with the team."

"Not with the team, with a player," added Rick, the pitching coach.

"Which, of course, affects the team," added Dave, rubbing his lip, an action which Megan had seen over the years.

She leaned forward, focusing on these decision-makers. "So, what can I do to help?"

"And if that isn't the perfect opening," said Dave.

"It's your show," said Scott Cohen. "I'm here only to observe. And report back to Harold. The club is not just a business to him. The man loves the game and takes an interest in every player we've got."

She nodded. The team's owner was famous for caring about every part of the organization, including the players. Maybe especially the players. But she still didn't know where this conversation was heading.

Rick started pacing. "As I said, we've got a player...a lot of talent, but..." He shook his head. "I'm not getting through to him."

"Then something's wrong," said Megan, "and not with you. My ear is to the ground. The pitching lineup appreciates you."

A glance passed between the two managers. "Told ya' she'd have a notion about it," said Dave. "She played women's softball at University of Texas. On scholarship, too. Made a name for herself. She knows the game."

A lump took root in her stomach as a pair of sparkling green eyes again came to mind. She glanced from the pitching coach to Dave, the team manager. Might as well throw the elephant into the room.

"Brian Delaney," she said.

She had fun watching their jaws drop. "Why are you surprised? He's just as unreliable for public events as he is on the mound. I obviously have no clout with him and am certainly out of ideas. Sorry." She began to rise.

Dave held up his hand like a traffic cop, and she sat down again. "Brian Delaney is either brilliant or a screw-up on the mound."

True. She'd watched enough games to see both. But could a pro team afford to have a clown in the lineup? Three pair of eyes were on her. "What?" she asked. "What can I do about him?"

"We think it's an attitude thing. Not a skill thing." Dave steepled his hands, elbows on the desk. "We want you to…to be his handler for the rest of the season. Figure out what makes him tick, get him to show up for every practice." The man didn't look too happy himself when he met her eyes. "Megan, the boss upstairs has a gut feeling about the kid."

Feelings. The sport was built on feelings. And performance, of course. She preferred the statistics route herself. "With all due respect to Mr. Weber, Brian Delaney was drafted out of college, so he's not a kid anymore, at least not in a baseball sense. At this point, have you considered trading him? If he's a problem that doesn't want to be solved, you might as well cut the team's losses."

Dave shook his head and leaned toward her from across his desk. "We need him right now. After last night's game, we're down to three starters. Damn tendinitis! We're calling up two players from the minors, of course, so we have our roster of five starting pitchers. Delaney's one of that five and the only left-handed one we have." He paused, stood and slapped the desk. "I repeat, we need him, Megan. It's either now or never. Can we develop him into all that he can be on the mound, as well as help the team maintain an honorable standing in the league?"

She was being pulled under. Hope and frustration swirled through the air. Heck, they were all frustrated. But the men were looking at her for hope.

"No technical training involved," said Rick. "I'll handle that, but with you in my corner, we might get different results."

"I-I'm not a miracle worker."

Dave opened a top drawer. "Your resume's right here. You're smart. You've played the game, you majored in psychology and communications..."

She held up her hand. "But I'm not a psychologist. I just love the game! But speaking of...has he spoken with the shrink yet? Our sports doc is really good. He knows how a ball player's mind works."

Dave's eyes fell. "He won't go. Says he doesn't have a problem. He's doing his job."

She jumped from her seat. "He won't go? Just like that? For crying out loud, fine him! Maybe if he'd stop cruising the clubs every night and get some sleep, it would help. Does he think he's Babe Ruth? That guy caroused, but when he played ball—he played to win!"

5

Pacing now, she wondered why she'd allowed her own emotions to kick in. Was it because she hated to see wasted talent, or something else?

"He's paid fines twice already, without an argument," said Rick quietly. "He's an untapped keg of potential. If I only had the key to…" his voice trailed off.

"We've invested a ton of money in him," said Scott, the general manager. "Either he comes through or I'll recommend cutting him." His gaze touched on each of them. "My job is telling Harold the facts and providing a well thought-out opinion. In the end, he'll make up his own mind."

"We don't want to cut him." Dave said immediately. He glanced at Megan, then looked away, then back at her. "There's one thing he does like," he said.

"Oh?"

"Yeah. He likes women. And he likes you."

"Women? I can believe." But liking her? Impossible. Brian Delaney didn't know she was even alive. "If the players like me, it's because I speak their language, and I don't waste their time." Her voice softened. "And believe me, I take their camaraderie as a big compliment. In general, the guys trust me. They come through at the hospitals, charity events…"

The three men nodded in unison, and Megan fought to hold back a chuckle at the sight. Just for the moment. The situation, itself, was not funny at all.

"We have a hunch, Megan, that you can pull this off," said Dave. "Rick and I would totally support you."

She studied each man now. They weren't kidding around. She had her career to consider. The possible promotion. And her reputation as a professional within the organization. Of course, soon her resume would read: *baby-sitter to spoiled brat, Brian Delaney.*

"A hunch?" she repeated. "Well then, that's the bottom line in our world, isn't it? Hunches, feelings, superstitions, jinxes, aligned planets, auras, and lots of woo-woo." She smiled to include herself in the observation. "I've lived with those 'hunches' all my life, too. And that fool does have oodles of talent."

"So, you're in?" asked Dave.

"Let's hope his womanizing doesn't apply to me— or I'm out."

"Agreed."

"By the way," said Scott, "speaking of bottom lines. Did we mention the bonus that goes along with this special assignment?"

She sat taller. "I'm all ears, my friends." A single mom never turned down a chance to earn overtime.

"Ten thou for the try, and another fifteen for the get. If you turn him around, Megan Ross, that's twenty-five thousand beyond salary and holiday bonus." The general manager was speaking for the owner. It seemed everyone was as serious as death about this 'assignment.'

She slowly exhaled the breath she'd been holding. Their generosity was nothing to sneeze at. Her ex was totally out of the picture. A real charmer with no sense of responsibility. Not unlike Delaney, she supposed.

"We would have mentioned it earlier," said Dave. "But we all played the same hunch on you, and we all won." His grin stretched across his face.

She chuckled and shook her head. "Might have known." More than ever, she felt at one with the organization. She'd earned their respect before doing a day's work with Delaney. Now she'd have to retain it.

##

Brian Delaney glanced at his watch as he ran up the five flights to Dave Evans's office. Three o'clock. And the game started at 7:05 that night. He took a moment to catch his breath at the top of the stairs, content with the timeframe. He'd be able to make a prearranged visit at the hospital and be back for pre-game warm up. After last night's trouble with Travis Watson's arm, Brian wanted to be in good form that night—for the team's sake—in case they needed him. Actually, Brian felt awful about Travis, too. No pitcher wanted to be laid up with tendinitis. He'd come through for a friend.

He jogged to Dave's office, called out a "yo" to Carla and stopped at the doorway to stare at the best pair of legs in Houston. So glad she often wore sundresses! Megan Ross not only had legs, she had a body, face and a personality to boot. The total package. He enjoyed rattling her.

"Hey, y'all," he said, after knocking on the door. "Is it a party?" He turned to Megan. "Good to see you…I think. Or am I in trouble again?" He paused. "Was there a photo shoot or something I missed?"

"Nope," she said, shaking her head, blonde hair swirling on her shoulders. "But we will be working together. Why don't you have a seat?" She turned to Dave. "You're up. Time to explain the plan."

Brian didn't like the look that passed between them, didn't like the sound of the word "plan." And he didn't like the four-to-one odds. He continued to stand near the doorframe and leaned against the wall. His hand went into a pocket of his baggy cargo shorts and cupped one of the baseballs he always had with him. A habit he'd acquired since moving to Houston.

As he listened to the "plan," he began to relax. It had to be a joke. He waited until Dave ran out of steam.

"And to think, my ears weren't even burning as you spent all this time talking about me," he began.

"Probably because you were just having fun. So, let's put it to rest. First of all, as lovely as Megan is, I don't need a baby-sitter. And second," he said, stepping further into the room, "baseball *is* about having fun! For the fans and the players."

If Dave Evans's eyes opened any wider, they'd pop out. "Do I look like I'm having fun?" the man growled.

"Well, maybe I can help you out there. Help you relax more." Brian took the ball out of his pocket, then reached for another and a third from the opposite pocket. He tossed one ball into the air, then added the second, then the last. For thirty seconds the room was silent as all eyes watched him juggle the three balls.

"God, his eye-hand coordination is fantastic," whispered Rick.

Brian smiled inside, kept juggling, and spoke. "I do take the game seriously. Check the stats. Don't I have the best record in the league for fewest stolen bases allowed?" Of course, he did. Catching runners was a hoot.

He heard mumbled agreement and juggled himself toward the door. "Sorry to break this up early, but I've got a date...with a very special lady." His heart squeezed for a moment as one by one, he caught each ball.

Turning at the doorway, he added, "I can't disappoint her." He jogged back to the stairwell.

##

Silence reigned for half-a-minute after Brian disappeared. Dave spoke first. "What just happened here? Does anyone know what just happened in here?"

"That was Brian being Brian," said Megan. "Doing what he always does—having fun."

"At whose expense?" asked Dave.

"And who's the special lady?" asked Megan. "Maybe she's the key to unlocking him."

"No girlfriends that I know of," said Rick. "And I'd probably know if there was someone."

"Ditto that," said Dave. "His whole family's back east though. His brother's with the Red Sox. Maybe we should've drafted him instead."

"We needed a pitcher, not a fielder," said Rick.

Interesting. She hadn't thought about his brother or his family, for that matter. She knew little about them, had never been curious. She knew the married players' wives and many of their children. They went to the games and most of the women played in the annual wives' softball game each year, which she coached. But as for the single guys…she didn't know much. They seemed more self-contained. Or maybe they just preferred keeping their private lives…private.

"I'll leave you three to figure out the details," said Scott, "and I'll brief Harold on our game plan." He turned to Megan. "Do your best, but don't make sacrifices you wouldn't ordinarily make."

"Huh?"

"You're part of the team, too, Megan. Play it safe." He waved and left the room.

"I'll second that. Delaney's a playboy, so keep your guard up," said Dave.

"You're concerned for nothing," said Megan. "I don't make the same mistakes twice."

"You've got a great kid, though," said Dave. "So that wasn't a mistake."

"My son," Megan began, and to her surprise, started choking up, "is the best child in the world." A new thought struck her about this assignment. "I need to keep Delaney away from Josh." She walked back and forth. "I'll have to figure out…"

Dave's hand went up again. "Slow down a minute. This whole project might not last very long at all. Think about Sandy Koufax. It took him six years — six years, Megan—before the whole game clicked for him and his brilliance on the mound showed up as no-hitters and perfect games. Brian Delaney is just about at that same point." He looked at her and shrugged his shoulders. "Maybe…?'

She tilted her head back. "From your mouth to God's ears, as my mom always says. With Delaney, we really will need divine help to perform an attitude adjustment or…should I say, a baseball miracle?"

"Ha! You're right. I hope you have a direct line to the bigger boss upstairs ."

CHAPTER TWO

Josh ran to Megan's car as she pulled to a stop in front of the YMCA. His counselor was right behind him, and Megan sighed with relief. Traffic had been awful—as usual.

She shut the engine and walked to the curb.

"Mom! You're late." Josh stood right in front of her now, head tilted back, waiting.

She leaned down, grabbed him for a hug and kiss. "I'm sorry, Josh, and sorry for being mushy, but I just love you, my boy."

"Yuck." He turned to the teen who'd accompanied him. "Sorry about her, Danny. She gets that way."

Megan threw back her head and laughed with pure joy. "Joshua Patrick Ross, you are the best medicine a person can have." She turned to the teen. "Thanks for staying with him. I'll try to get here sooner tomorrow."

"You say that every day, Ms. Ross," said Danny. "But Josh is a good kid, so no problem."

She studied the teen for a moment as an idea surfaced. "I think you're a good kid, too, Danny, and I'm wondering if you have any free time in the evenings to stay with Josh if I have to work late."

His brow furrowed.

"Whatever the going rate is...I'm good," she added.

"It's just that I'm playing in Senior League, so I'd have to check my schedule."

"Fair enough," she said. "What position?"

"Pitcher."

She sighed and mumbled under her breath, *might have known.*

But with a smile for Danny, she said, "See you tomorrow."

"And mom, be on time!" pleaded Josh.

"I guess you don't like being the last one picked up, huh?" she offered, once they were both in her reliable Honda Civic.

"No offense, but I think you might forget."

Her heart almost stopped as she turned and cupped Josh's face in her hands. She looked into big blue eyes just like her own. "Never," she said. "That will never, ever happen. I love you too much for that."

"Okay. Can we go to MacDonald's?"

And just like that, the topic changed. His eight-year-old brain was off and running to other things.

"No fast food, and besides, Pops and Grandma are expecting us tonight."

"Oh, good. Swimming."

Her mom and stepfather had splurged and put an in-ground pool in their backyard, which was a big hit with Josh and his cousins. Megan suspected the pool was Grandma's bait to keep her house full of family. Smart woman. And smart Megan, too, for eventually buying a house in her mom's neighborhood. It had taken a while after her divorce to figure things out, but with a bit of help with a down payment, Megan had become a homeowner in a family-centered community about a half-hour from work—on good days.

She pulled into the driveway next to Craig's car, which meant both parental units were home. Josh grabbed his camp bag and flew to the front door, Megan right behind him.

"Hello, hello," she called. And suddenly, the kitchen was full of people. Her nephew, Trevor, was also there. "Hi, squirt," she said, mussing his hair. "Parents not here?"

His nose wrinkled. "Nope. They're taking Sam to a *princess* movie. Do you think I wanted to go?"

Oh, the tone of his voice, the look on his face! Young boys could keep her in stitches. "I don't suppose so. And perhaps Samantha would prefer to have their undivided attention, hmm?"

"She can have it. C'mon Josh. Let's go swimming."

"Not until I get there," she warned.

"I'll go with them." Craig Fanning leaned over and kissed her on the brow. "How was your day, sweetheart?"

She thought back over the last hour or so and shook her head. "You wouldn't believe it, Pops. I'll tell you later." She glanced at her watch. "But I'll need to catch the game at seven."

"Twist my arm, kiddo. I'll be sitting right next to you." He waved and headed toward the backyard with the boys. And the kitchen was quiet.

"Whew," said Megan, turning toward her mom. "Can I make a salad or something? How can I help?"

"Sure, and set the table, too. If we're all watching a game in less than an hour, we'd better eat soon."

She worked quickly and quietly on her light chores and called the "men" in to change clothes. When the boys disappeared to their usual bedroom in Grandma's house, Megan got her folks' attention.

"Now that we're alone, I need to tell you about a new assignment because I might need backup help with Josh. There's a big bonus attached, so…" She saw them nod their heads.

"Craig gets home by six every night, and I'm home by five, so we're here for you. I can even pick Josh up at camp at the end of the day."

Once more, they'd stand behind her, providing strong backup, as they'd done through her divorce and aftermath when she fought for total custody—and got it. "Thank you," she whispered, "for just being you."

And then she told them about Brian Delaney and watched her mom's expression turn to one of horror.

"You'll be spending a lot of time with a-a-playboy? What are you thinking? If you need money, we'll help you. No, Megan. No more irresponsible charmers who walk away from everything that counts. We've been through that once already." She turned to Craig, lifted her chin, then turned back to Megan. "In fact, twice. Your own father was the same. You and I have both made the same mistake. No more."

Megan almost crumbled. She took her mom in her arms. "This time I'm forewarned. And it's business, Mom. Not social. I've got all of management behind me. Dave Evans, Rick Marinelli, Scott Cohen, the general manager. And even Harold Weber, the owner. Everyone…"

"I don't care about everyone! Will they be with you when you're in his apartment alone? Will they be with you when you're 'building a rapport' with

16

him…whatever the heck that means? He's a spoiled brat!"

She appealed to her stepfather. "Craig, you know the talent that man has…explain to her."

"If he has such talent," said Craig, "it's his call to hone it and use it. No one can force him, and I can't predict his choice." He stepped to his wife and held her in his arms, her back against his chest. "Kathy, my love—Meggie is not that naïve youngster she once was. She's made good choices since then. I guess being a mom will do that. I trust her."

Kathy twirled. "I trust her too, but I worry. It's *him* I don't trust at all!"

If it weren't serious for her, Megan would have laughed. But she did need to calm her mom, so laughing was out. "Let's be fair. None of us really know him, so let's not judge him yet." Of course, she'd already found him wanting, but…

"I'm going to give it my best shot," she said. "We're down to only three regular starters plus the two called up, and Delaney just has to come through."

##

He'd turned his performance up a notch that night, helping the 'Stros to a 4-1 win, striking out every player in the oppositions' lineup at least once. Maybe that would take the pressure off for a while.

Once changed into street clothes after a massage and shower in the locker room, he called out a general good night and started to leave.

"Good game, Delaney."

"Yeah. Take care of that arm. We sure don't need any more starters on the injured list."

Brian waved. "I hear ya' and one hundred percent agree. It's the treadmill for me tomorrow."

The camaraderie among the guys was a balm to his spirits after that meeting in Dave's office. He'd always been a social-type person, more so than his twin brother. He didn't want to let anyone down, but heck, he wanted to have a fun time, too. "It's late. Anyone need a ride? Or want to stop off at a watering hole?"

"You just pitched seven friggin' innings, man. Go home and rest."

He waved and left. Home. He'd been in his condo for almost four years. Was it a home? He called it "the apartment." Sure, it had space and a great location not far from the park. A decorator had put some furniture in it. He shrugged and headed to his car. He was on his own in H-Town, as the locals called Houston. No family nearby, and he still missed not being around them. Maybe he really hadn't grown up. Maybe he shouldn't need his family so much anymore.

His cell phone buzzed as he got behind the wheel. Megan Ross. He felt a frisson of anticipation, and his melancholy thoughts disappeared. This should be good.

"Yo, Megan."

"Good game tonight, Brian. And I truly mean it."

"That does happen from time to time," he retorted as he placed the phone in its holder and started the engine.

"Yes, yes it does. A great pitcher is a beautiful thing to watch."

Complimenting him already? Softening him up? But sincerity lined her voice, and suddenly, he was tired of the one-upmanship game. "Let's not go overboard. Thanks for the approval. Now what can I do for you...seeing as you've rarely called me after a game."

"Okay then, down to business. I'd like to get together with you, basically review your schedule and set up a couple of dates when we can visit."

"You've got to be kidding. That business in Dave's office this morning couldn't be serious."

"Wrong, Brian. I'm as serious as the business end of a .45."

He emitted a long, low whistle. "Texas born and bred, huh? Well, put this into your ten-gallon: Brian Delaney doesn't scare easily."

"Okay, maybe I came on too strong. But listen up. We're both earning our salaries with the team, and they want us to try. You were there today. You know it."

"I'm pulling out of the parking lot now and need to maneuver. Just give me a minute."

"Sure."

The fans had gone by now, and traffic was light. He wanted to buy time. The woman had a point. He was earning a ton of money, so maybe he owed some cooperation. He hadn't really looked at it from that angle before. Maybe the situation could be worse. After all, Megan Ross was a looker. And single. And smart. He loved smart. Was used to smart. His sisters…every one of them outstandingly smart and talented in different ways. He started to smile. All's fair in love and war. Wasn't that the saying?

"So are y'all declarin', Tex, that we're stuck with each other?" he asked in the best drawl he could produce, while tamping down his light Boston accent.

Her chuckle made him smile. "That's one way of putting it."

He wasn't going to make it too easy though. "Well, Ms. Lone Star, in that case, I'm all yours. Anytime, anyplace. You need a little enjoyment in your life."

"Oh, for heaven's sake, Delaney. Save it for the bar bimbos. Doesn't work with me."

"*We've only just begun…*" he sang softly.

"Right. So how does tomorrow morning at ten sound? You can sleep in for a bit."

The woman was all business every time. "You're the boss," he said, deciding to humor her.

"I'll believe that when pigs fly...or you pitch a no-hitter."

She was baiting him. Already on the job even before they met. "I'll leave the key with the doorman in the morning. I'll be out running."

"Don't forget to finish back at home."

That word was haunting him tonight. But even an elite athlete couldn't run all the way to Massachusetts. "How can I possibly forget, Ms. Megan, when you'll be waiting for me?"

"You're impossible. I don't know whether to laugh or cry, so I'll say goodnight." And she hung up.

Brian chuckled, content that he'd gotten her off-balance. She needed to be shaken up. She needed some excitement. And he was very good at providing it. In more than three years, he'd never seen her without a million papers on her desk, a million phone calls, always running around and giving orders. Getting things done. And then going home. He'd noticed all that...and more. Those legs, a killer smile and a body—straight and tall, strong, shapely...hmm...very shapely.

Oh, yeah. Megan Ross had been on his radar for a long time. He'd always waved and winked when they'd crossed paths. But he'd never broken his rule about socializing only outside the workplace. No woman was worth complications on the job.

It seemed that now, however, was the right time for that principle to be tested.

##

Megan stopped off for two large cups of coffee on her way to Brian's place the next morning. Might as well start out with a peace offering. She pictured chatting at a kitchen table, sipping the joe, getting to know each other. If he had a kitchen table. Sometimes these high-end apartments had galley kitchens only. The tenants here ate out a good deal. Or ordered in.

She found a parking spot only a block away. Must be her lucky day. When she approached the building, the doorman greeted her with keys.

"Mr. Delaney said he's only doing three miles this morning, so he'll be back sooner than he thought."

"Thank you, Mr...." —she peered at his I.D.— "Gardner. I appreciate the message."

"It's the fourth floor," the man added.

"Thanks again."

"He's a good fellow, a good man."

Chatty guy. She paused and looked him in the eye. "Did he ask you to give him a reference?"

"No, ma'am. All he said was the brass was comin'. Guess that means you."

She grinned. "Mr. Gardner, you don't have to worry about me. I'm no brass. I'm just a working stiff like everybody else."

Had Brian thought he'd need to gather allies against her invasion? She stepped toward the open door, called out a thanks and made her way toward the elevators. She passed a small reception area with a desk, noted the mirrored walls in the lobby, along with decorative plants and a couple of leather club chairs. Lovely tiered-glass chandeliers provided soft light.

Whew. Like a small hotel. Except some people called the building home. She pressed the fourth-floor button and barely felt the usual anti-gravity pull as the car quietly rose. She couldn't imagine the amount of rent Brian was paying to live here, but that part was certainly not her business.

From his doorway, she scanned the living-dining room combination and the entrance to the kitchen.

Closing the door behind her, she headed to the kitchen first and halted at the entrance. Wow! She'd been totally wrong about it. Large, with an island and an expanse of counter space that made her envious. An eating alcove nested in the corner. After depositing the coffee and her purse on the table, she walked back into the living area and turned in a slow circle. Very contemporary, with glass tables, leather sofa, and area rug. A wall unit held a television, wine rack, and some kind of built-in stereo system. On the wall, a couple of modern art pieces. The room was surprisingly neat and clean.

Neat, clean…and cold. Not a shred of his personality showed. Where was the quick smile, gleaming eyes, and warmth of the man? Not even a stack of books or magazines to be seen. Not even sports magazines. Well, maybe he had no time to read. She walked down an adjacent hallway toward the back and passed a laundry room, bathroom and finally the master bedroom. Ahh — too personal. Retracing her steps, she noticed a partly open door to a room opposite the kitchen. Maybe for visiting guests?

She gently pushed it open and stepped into Brian's world.

Astro team pictures lined the left wall, going back five years. Megan walked closer and examined each one, nodding and recognizing the whole lot of them. On the wall opposite the door—the photos a visitor saw first—were shots of the great left-handed pitchers and Cy Young award winners. Sandy Koufax, Warren Spahn, Brian Carlton, Tom Glavine. Complementing that group was right-hander, Don Larsen, who pitched a perfect World Series game in 1956. Totally unexpected magic.

Megan felt a smile splash across her face. Excitement rose inside her. This was what she'd needed to know in order to understand him. And she wasn't finished. A worn-looking couch rested against the third wall and on the table before it sat a bottle of linseed oil, three gloves each wrapped around a ball and tied closed, a couple of batting gloves and wrist sweatbands. Nearby stood a rack of bats, a half-dozen pair of spikes and rubber cleats. The epitome of a boy scout — always prepared.

The Game Room. The heart of his home. For a first visit to his place, she'd discovered a great deal. The game did mean something to Brian, which might make it easier for their relationship. She loved the game, too. These initial peeks into his life made her more curious. What else did he keep hidden away from casual eyes? Why did he pretend not to care about the game, when he obviously did? Why did he maintain such a cavalier attitude about everything? The world wasn't a joke, Brian!

Brian Delaney was a mystery she wanted to solve.

LINDA BARRETT

CHAPTER THREE

Sweating, but breathing easily, Brian let himself into the apartment and called out Megan's name.

"Right here," she said, waving her arm from the sofa. She stood and smiled at him, looking refreshingly cool in one of those sleeveless dresses she usually wore with the flared skirt. He glanced at her legs. Yup, just like he remembered. Long, shapely and perfect.

"You'll be happier if I shower first," he joked and headed toward his master suite.

She waved him away while holding her nose in a jocular manner. "Go, go."

The woman was finally relaxed, in a good mood-- and looking very pretty that way. They hadn't even chatted yet, and he wondered at the change in her demeanor. If he could figure it out, he'd have her feeling good all the time, and this "special project" would end quickly. Unless…it turned out that he enjoyed himself. If that happened, all bets were off.

Ten minutes later, he invited her for brunch in his own kitchen, the room that sold him on the apartment. Kitchens had happy memories, and besides, he needed both pantry and work space.

"Let's mix up the carbs and the protein." He reached into a drawer for two pans and set them to heat. "Eggs, turkey bacon, whole wheat bread. Crack, fry, toast." Suiting action to words, he hummed as he worked, flipping the eggs, turning the bacon, and reaching for plates and silverware in split-second timing.

"I'll do the cleanup," Megan offered. "It's the least I can do for this treat. You're like a professional chef— the prep, movements, timing. In fact, you move in the kitchen like you do on the field. Smooth and-and silky."

Silky? A weird word to use on a pitcher? Silky is what her skin looked like. Pure honey. His busy hands itched to pause and stroke her cheek. He took a deep breath instead.

"Thanks, I guess. I'm happy in the kitchen," he said, "but it's also good to eat in the clubhouse with the guys."

"More fun too, I'd guess. Do you ever feel lonely here?"

He glanced at her. It was a serious question, no gotcha in it. "Everyone gets lonely once in a while, don't you think?"

Her answer came slowly. "If I disagreed, I'd be a liar, but I think some people feel it more often than others."

"Well, we're not lonely now, so sit down and eat." Good deflection. He wasn't in the mood for "serious" this early in the morning. He placed the food on the table.

She glanced at the plates and burst out laughing. "Thanks for trying to be fair, but there's no way I can eat all this."

The stacks of food looked normal to him.

"Do you mind?" She stood, went to the cabinet and retrieved another plate. Scooping half her food onto it, she said, "You can have a snack later on."

Her smile warmed him, and her eyes bubbled with humor. He liked this version of Megan Ross much better than the one at work.

"Are you coming to the game tonight?" he asked between bites.

"Not unless you're pitching. And you're not. So, the answer's no. I have an eight-year-old son, so weekend games work better for me."

He nodded. "I've met Josh a time or two. Cute. And a good kid."

She dimpled. "The best. He's at baseball camp this summer, and of course, he loves the game."

"Then he must take after his mother."

Her eyes darkened. "Thank God for that."

Touched a nerve there, hadn't he? "I think Josh is a lucky kid."

She tilted her head and looked at him curiously. "What do you mean?"

He leaned back in his chair, took a sip of coffee. "Well...what if your passion had been crochet? Huh? What would he have done then?"

In two seconds, her laughter filled his kitchen. He watched her grab her stomach. "You always go for a laugh, Brian, but this one was really good. Crochet? I don't even know how to hold the needle. Or hook. Or whatever it is."

He had her where he wanted her, relaxed and happy. The perfect time to strike. "So, Megan, let's get down to business. What are you doing tomorrow night?"

Her thoughts raced. She had to admit, he was a step ahead of her now. The next day's game was at 1:10 pm, and he wasn't pitching. He would certainly be free for the evening.

"I'll be at home with my son…unless something comes up at work." Which it often did, but hopefully, not this time. She needed some normal down time with Josh.

"Hmm…"

She watched him think. His head nodded, his eyes gleamed. She was starting to like him. Oops. Caution. Caution. An ache started in the pit of her stomach.

"Here's the deal, Meggie," he finally said. "Your goal is to get to know me better. My goal is to get to know you better. Now, we may have different reasons, but it can't happen if we're apart." He paused. "Make sense?"

"Not with Josh. My son's off limits."

His eyes widened, his nostrils flared. "What the hell do you think I'm going to do to him? I like kids."

She reached over and squeezed his hand in apology. "I know you do," she said, "but then you'll disappear." She took a breath. "I won't let that happen to my son again."

He flipped his wrist and captured her soft hand within his. Then looked her in the eye and said, "Are you sure you're worried only about Josh?"

She pulled away. The best defense was an offense, and she wasn't shy. With her fingers gripping the edge of the table, she said, "I'm not the one in the spotlight here. It's not my life that's giving the club fits. It's yours."

"And I'm not concerned." He raised his eyes to what appeared to be a family photo, hanging on the wall, and studied it. "I do what I can and whatever happens, happens. No biggie. It's not like it's life or death."

The tone of his voice alerted her. Quiet. Solemn. If she'd had a highlighting marker, she'd rub it across that sentence. A reveal. A big one. "Are you speaking literally, Brian?" she asked softly.

"What do you think?"

"Don't play games with me now."

He pointed at the photo—a smiling man and woman—obviously a loving couple. "Meet my folks, Meggie. That's Grace and Robert Delaney. Sorry you can't shake their hands. They died when I was nine."

Her breath caught; her heart almost stopped. Why hadn't she researched his background before coming here? Rising slowly from her chair, she walked to the picture of his parents. "Beautiful couple. You've got your dad's looks, those shiny green eyes, the wave to your hair." She heard the tremolo in her voice, felt herself blink several times but swallowed her tears. She turned back to him. "I'm so very sorry, Brian. So unfair."

"Hey," he said, joining her. "It was a long time ago." He rubbed his thumb across her cheek. "I'm sorry, too. I didn't mean to slam you."

His light touch on her face, the warmth in his voice...all felt sincere. But... "Maybe you didn't, and maybe you did." She laid her hand over his and stepped back. "But you've gotten my attention." She took a deep breath. "Let's give ourselves a do-over. Let's start again."

His brow rose and he stood as still as she'd ever seen him. "I'm listening."

"While it's not life or death on the grand scale," she said, with a glance at the photo, "we are both still here on earth. An awful lot of people are depending on you. And, yes, I know it's a load of pressure. What can I do to help?"

For a moment, she thought he wouldn't answer. A quiet moment that stretched so long, she'd turned to leave.

"Just be in my corner, Megan. My three sisters and twin brother — we all have each others' backs. Supportive. Strong. I sure don't see you as another sister, but the loyalty factor...? That's necessary. How hard can it be?"

It would be easy to give in to him. He was a nice guy, and today with her, not the wise guy he'd been when showing off in Dave's office. But she had to be truthful.

"I'll be in your corner one hundred percent," she said, "if you'll be in mine."

Deep in thought when she left Brian's place, Megan almost missed the employees' parking lot entrance. *Get a grip, Meg.* The man had hidden depths, was more complex and insightful than she'd given him credit for. That crack he'd made keeping him away only to protect Josh had hit a target. She'd kept them all away! Every eligible guy on the team would have loved to get into her pants. She'd learned that during her first year on the job. But she'd also learned to handle their flirting with good-natured humor, and they got the message. So, yeah. She'd held them all at arm's length not only to protect Josh, but to protect herself.

"The best lessons are the hard lessons," she mumbled, as she took the elevator to the fourth floor and made a beeline to her office. Her normal responsibilities couldn't be ignored. Within twenty minutes, however, Dave Evans popped his head in.

"How's it going so far?"

She had to laugh. It had been less than one day since they'd discussed Brian. "I met him at his place this morning—after his three-mile run."

"Good, good. The day after pitching should be an easy one." He stepped inside. "And...?"

She leaned back in her chair, gathering her thoughts. "There's hope," she said, "but it's a little complicated." How much did she need to reveal about Brian's parents and the aftermath? "He has a room devoted to the outstanding left-handers of all time. Pictures, books, posters. He's got three gloves of his own oiled and wrapped up like babies in their blankets."

"I knew it!" Dave's grin echoed his sentiments. "I knew he loved it deep down. What's holding him back?"

"I'm working on that, but he has to trust me first. And trust takes time to build." Hint. Hint.

"You're doing great, Megan. Just keep me posted." He waved and left, a jaunty spring in his step.

She stared after him. If Dave was expecting her to perform miracles, he'd better think twice. But it was amazing what a little hope could do.

She picked up the receiver and called Human Resources. "Hey, Donna. What can you tell me about Brian Delaney? Background? Family? I'd appreciate anything you've got that you can legally divulge." She paused. "Ok. Thanks."

With all the privacy laws, she didn't expect much new information, probably not much more than available to the general public, but it was worth a shot.

Her phone rang and immediately Megan was lost in work, arranging player events, including a visit to Texas Children's Hospital and a morning meet-and-greet for season ticket holders.

Donna's call-back provided nothing new. Brian was raised in Boston, graduated from the University of

Miami, and was drafted out of college by the Red Sox organization, where he played Triple A for almost four years before being traded to Houston. Listed his next of kin as Andrew Delaney, brother.

"Right. They're twins. His brother is a power hitter for Boston, isn't he?" asked Megan.

"One and the same. In fact, they're identical twins. Maybe that's something you didn't know. And something all baseball fans across the country probably did know."

"Thanks, Donna. You're right. I guess I'm a very bad detective."

She slowly hung up the receiver, her thoughts racing. Brian had experienced painful separations in his life. Playing light and loose probably seemed safer to him. He was friendly with everyone, but had no close friends, at least not in Houston. Even if her hunches were right, however, what could she do about it?

Not a darn thing. She wasn't ready to sacrifice herself for the sake of Brian Delaney.

##

Megan watched the game on television that night. Brian wasn't playing, of course, but he was in uniform, and she caught glimpses of him in the dugout. It gave her a better understanding of the players if she watched them at work. Every single one of them was her client...in a way. A good rapport helped her get their cooperation, which made events much more fun and successful.

After the ninth inning, she turned off the TV and quietly walked into Josh's room. Sprawling across the mattress and breathing lightly, he looked so adorable. He'd made it through five innings before conking out. She leaned down and brushed a kiss on his forehead. Her little man. Her sweet boy.

She turned down the hall to her own room just as a text came in on her cell. Brian.

Still up?
Watched the game, kissed Josh goodnight. He's out cold.
Lucky kid to have you as his mom.

That man knew how to push the right button.

Hope he feels that way when he's grown. What do you need?
Nothing. Just checking up on you. See you tomorrow.

He disconnected.

Checking up on her? It was the other way around. She was the one assigned to keep watch over him. Hard to do that from a distance. Maybe she should have accepted his invitation for the following night, after the game.

She waited until the next day when he'd be in the complex before sending another message. His reply was promising.

I'll stop by as soon as I can.

She hadn't asked him to visit in person. A text would have been sufficient, but an hour later, when she'd almost finished creating a working calendar for the two of them, she sensed a presence at her door.

His hair was mussed, he carried his glove. "At your service, Meggie. What's up?"

"How's the workout?"

"Just playing some catch," he said, his green eyes gleaming as he pulled a ball out of his pocket to show her and stepped further inside her office.

She chuckled. "I bet you are…let's see, it's Day 2 after you pitched. So maybe some slow bullpen work, huh? Maybe only fifty or sixty miles an hour?"

"Don't know, never liked having an exact plan, but my arms feel good." He stretched both overhead, turned his torso left and right, before straightening out again. With every move, his jersey tightened, outlining an expanse of rippling muscle.

For a moment, she lost track of the conversation, then hoped her fair skin wouldn't turn pink and give her thoughts away.

"Jogged around the bases, too," he added. "You looking for a full report? Ask Rick."

"Nope," she said, taking a calming breath. "I'm not planning to go around you." She pointed to a chair. "Sit for a minute. I need you to trust me, so you know that I'm really in your corner."

His brows lifted. "I guess you listened last night." A wide grin appeared. "I'm glad you've decided not to be a spy."

"A spy?" She laughed. "Don't be so dramatic. It's not like that at all. Everyone cares. We're all pulling for you."

He stretched his legs out and leaned back. "Is that what you really believe? Baseball's a business, Megan. They—" he waved his hand toward the fifth-floor executive offices "—don't care about me as a person. In fact, no one knows a damn thing about me. They care about the numbers—the runs, errors, the stats. I'm just one of the bigger cogs in the wheel that can make the crowd happy on some days."

She picked up a pencil and started tapping it on her desk. "That is one of the saddest viewpoints I've ever heard from any player about this game. And you're wrong. The players care about you. You've got friends on the team. And if you think you don't, then whose fault is that?" Her voice rose, then she jumped to her feet and started pacing. "I've seen you be the life of a party here. And you've got such a good heart. How did you get so cynical?"

He was silent for such a long while, she thought he wasn't going to answer. But then she heard him softly say, "There's safety in numbers, Megan. Nothing lasts. People come and go, and sometimes they disappear." His bright green eyes became so shadowed, they looked almost black.

She swallowed a painful breath. He was referring to his folks, but she could apply his words to why she kept Josh away from anyone she dated. She was not in a position to throw stones.

Stepping from behind her desk, she pulled up another chair, and sat down next to him, their knees almost touching. "Have you ever considered a different set of statistics?" she asked quietly. "Like the tiny, tiny likelihood that a tragedy of that magnitude could strike twice?"

A wry smile appeared. "My math skills are excellent. My life skills may not be. I'm not taking any chances." He gathered his long legs under him and stood. "Are we done here?"

Were they? "I-I don't know. I don't even know how this conversation got so off-track."

This time when he laughed, the sound was filled with lightness and good humor. "I'm starting to make an exception with you," he said. "I'm beginning to like you more."

"Funny you should say that, since I'm actually starting to like you more, too." Even though he was absolutely more complicated than she'd thought he was last night. "And now I remember what I wanted to ask you in the first place." She had his attention, but suddenly found herself stammering her words. "Umm...I...ah...changed my mind about later on, if you're still available."

She saw his response before he spoke a word and was surprised at how disappointed she felt.

"As it turns out, I need to be home tonight. There's a livestream concert that I have to watch. In fact, I cannot, in all good conscience, miss it."

"Livestream? Must be something unique. What kind of music?"

His gaze challenged her. "Classical. And I don't mean classic country or rock."

She had no words for a moment. Her jaw simply dropped. "Well, you just rocked me out of orbit." Leaning back in her chair, she felt a smile emerge. "You are full of surprises, Brian Delaney. And I mean good ones! Or at least, interesting ones."

"I'm just keeping you on your toes and in my corner."

Nodding, she said, "So far, so good."

"So, how'd you like to join me this evening? I think you'll find the concert particularly interesting."

CHAPTER FOUR

As Brian suggested, for this visit she turned into the building's adjoining garage and found a guest spot on the first level. He was waiting for her and jogged over.

"Didn't want you to get lost," he said.

She held up her cell. "Always a back-up plan. But thank you."

He led her inside and gestured to the elevators. "Ride or stairs?"

Peering up at him, she said, "If this is a trick question, I cry uncle. We're riding up--what is it now— five flights? Just add it to your workout tomorrow."

"Count on it," he said with a chuckle, as he slipped through the sliding door.

The television in the living room was already on. "Has it started already?" Megan asked.

"Nope. Just making sure I'm connected. Which I am." He glanced at his watch. "Only a few more minutes. So, how did you get away tonight?"

"Josh is at my mom's. I'll pick him up for camp in the morning. He—ah—almost pitched a fit when he knew I was going to see you without bringing him." She glanced up quickly. "I had to tell him, because he really likes me to be home every night, and visiting you qualified as special. He does need a routine, though. All kids do."

"Why are you looking at me as if I minded? I don't mind at all."

"Well...I promised him that the next time he came to the stadium, you'd have a catch with him." She peeked at him again. "Just a short one would be fine." She sighed. "How did this all happen when I was trying so hard to keep work and home separate? Ugh!"

Brian's laugher was no help. "You are very cute when confused. And I would be happy to have a catch."

"At two miles an hour, Brian. Can you hold back like that? He's only eight years old." The protective mom had definitely made an appearance.

"Believe it or not, Meggie, I was once eight years old, too. My dad had double work throwing to Andy and me in the back yard. Until, of course, we had our own catches." He checked his watch again and reached for the TV controller. "Good times for all of us."

He didn't seem sad at all, his memory as natural as anyone else's. "It sounds like family fun. For Josh's sake, I have to admit I'm glad to have the background and skill set to be a good partner for him. I'm glad I'm not a wimp."

"You?" he asked, his eyes wide as he pointed at her. "You're anything but a wimp. I like that. I'm used to strong women around me. Although..."

She waited.

"Let's wait and see." He waved her to the sofa and sat down next to her. "I hope we connect."

On the screen a moment later, Megan saw crowds of people on blankets, lawn chairs and in the distance, more attendees inside the venue. Across the top of the screen was displayed *Tanglewood Music Center.* Her mind kicked into overdrive.

Brian was from Massachusetts and Tanglewood was the summer home of the Boston Symphony Orchestra. Maybe he just wanted to connect with a piece of home. Or maybe an old friend was in the audience. She sat back, ready to enjoy whatever music was performed. Brian sat forward, elbows on knees, his breathing erratic.

Within moments, the host and hostess of the program welcomed everyone attending in person as well as the livestream audience, talked about the wonderful summer programs at the venue, and finally began introducing the program.

"It's about time," growled Brian, glancing at Megan. "Hang in a moment longer, Meggie, and you'll see and hear."

"Playing Tchaikovsky's Violin Concerto in D Major, accompanied by the Boston Symphony, is a Tanglewood alumna, former Fellow and recently returned from a European tour, violinist, Ms. Emily Delaney,"

"Delaney?" she whispered.

"My kid sister. She's branched out. Mozart used to be her fave."

His sister? Her hand flew to her chest. Had she heard him correctly? Megan leaned forward, too, watching in disbelief. A petite brunette, in a simple dark pink summer dress, carrying a violin and bow, took her place as the audience applauded in welcome. The young woman turned to the conductor and nodded.

For the next thirty-five minutes, Megan allowed herself to be immersed in the most beautiful music she'd ever heard. Some parts seemed familiar, but the emotions it evoked from extreme highs to pensive lows simply carried her away.

"Wait for it," Brian whispered at the end, during the applause. "I think—she always—never grew out of—" His lips pressed together as he continued watching.

Once more, his sister raised the violin and bow. The familiar strains of *Amazing Grace* filled the room while absolute silence marked the audience's respect. As if they knew something...

Grace. His mother. Her mother. Megan recalled her name from the photo in his kitchen. That long-ago accident must have left its mark on the musical child-turned-adult, too. Her hunch had been correct. This audience did know. Their enthusiastic applause certainly supported her.

"So, Brian..." she asked with a smile, "do you have any other surprises for me?"

"You never know," he replied standing up just as his phone rang. He checked the readout and grinned. "Lisa! You were there? You and Mike? Yeah, she was great. Too bad Andy had a game tonight. I'll call him later." He paused as he listened. "I have no idea who'd send her that many flowers. Maybe it was Andy because he couldn't watch?" He chatted a bit more, disconnected and turned to her.

"And this is one way the Delaneys keep in touch. Ball games, concerts and...other stuff as well." He led the way to the kitchen.

She reached out and squeezed his arm. "You may not be an ordinary family, Brian, but from what you said the other night, the Delaney siblings manage to be there for each other when it's important."

He stared into her eyes, and she couldn't turn away. "'Manage' is about all we do, Meggie. Crazy schedules. Emily flying everywhere. Mike, Andy and I traveling to games. Living apart. I'd give my last dollar to live the life of that ordinary family you mentioned."

She paused before replying, thinking about that concept "I wonder if there is one? Does an ordinary family exist other than in our imaginations?"

"Oh, c'mon. Don't get too philosophical. Aren't there millions of moms and dads with two kids?" He went to the freezer and extracted two half-gallons of ice cream. "Perfect on a summer's night, eh?"

Without thinking twice, she reached into his dish cupboard for bowls. "And I adore mint-chocolate-chip! I'm usually the only one who does. What a great coincidence."

"If you want to think so…"

She needed a second. "How did you know?"

"I pay attention to details. At events or at games, you always go for the mint chocolate chip when there's ice cream around."

She thought back through the past year to the number of receptions, promotions, visits, and formal dinners with supporters. She'd certainly been at a load of home games. "I'll have to run bases if I keep eating so much ice cream," she said as she popped a spoonful into her mouth.

"No chance! You're perfect the way you are."

She shook her head and laughed. "You're good for my ego, but you're so wrong. For starters, my choices in men stink, and in case it hasn't registered with you, I also do not come from an ordinary family."

His eyes narrowed, and he leaned in. "Tell me, Megan. Now that we have this rapport growing…"

Maybe she should. Her goal was to build trust with him. He wasn't going to blab her background to all the guys on the team. Anyway, they already knew she was a single mom. She took another spoonful of ice cream, and slowly raised her head to meet his gaze.

"Here's the summary: my dad was a happy-go-lucky charmer whom I adored. He walked out on us when I was eight and my brother was eleven. He attracted women the way flowers attract bees. My mom did her best, but I was inconsolable. I loved being his 'princess.'"

"Geez, doesn't every little girl want that? I'm sorry, Meggie."

"But the worst part, Brian, is that I chose the exact same kind of man as my mom did. So, there you have it. Josh's dad walked out and gave up legal claim to him when our son was six months old. Josh's last name is Ross, just like mine. And of course, child support is non-existent. Therefore, my job is crucial to us."

He nodded. "I get that. And now I'm part of your responsibilities, giving you another headache."

"I thought so too, in the beginning, but I'm changing my mind. You're not so bad. I'm glad they didn't trade you when I suggested it."

"You what?" His voice rose at least five notes.

"I told them to cut their losses." She leaned forward, her eyes challenging him. "And why not?" She began ticking off reasons on her fingers. "You haven't been reliable on the mound, you're not organized, you spend too many nights clubbing around… On any given day you can be brilliant, and then can't even find the plate." She took a breath. "They're paying you oodles of money, Brian, and they want a winning team. But if we don't win, it should be because another team is truly better. And not because we're sloppy." She heaved a sigh. "Boy, I could use a drink."

"Does that mean you're done with your analysis?"

Maybe she'd gone overboard. "I'm nowhere near perfect either, but I try my best." She leaned across the table toward him. "Can you just focus on finding the plate? Make an honest effort?"

His pause seemed an hour long. It was only seconds.

"An honest effort? The team's league standing is in the top half. I'm doing my part while keeping my mental balance which requires a social life. Or some distractions. Do you get that?"

"Of course I understand the need for a balanced life! Not that I'm the model for one...

Sighing, she looked squarely at him and gave it her best shot. "We both know that pitching is the most valuable commodity in baseball. I know you're under tremendous pressure, but for better or worse, it's on you and the other starters. And I'm so sorry to be the messenger. Maybe you should've played center field."

She stood and searched for her purse. "I'll go now."

"Not yet, please, Megan. Sit down and have more ice cream. You can relax. I'm not going to kill this particular messenger." His quick smile did slow her exit. "And by the way, my brother plays center field. I've always been a pitcher."

She plopped into the chair, felt him sizing her up.

"I don't know what you're going to tell the top brass about me," he said, "but I do know how you can make your own case."

"I don't have a ....

"Tell them you entered the lion's den and survived."

Her laughter started from deep down inside and bubbled up to the surface. "I did, didn't I?"

His eyes gleamed as he nodded. Was it admiration she saw?

"Just FYI — I use my own judgment with the brass. So have a good night's sleep."

##

Two mornings later, Dave walked into Megan's office, worry lines across his brow. His mouth was pressed into a thin line.

"Just a heads-up. Delaney's pitching tonight, a day ahead of schedule." He began pacing as he spoke. "Bad luck is stalking the starting roster. Again. Jimmy Williams was in a car accident last night on his way home after the game. Says it's minor. Do I believe him? His car is totaled."

She let him talk. He was a manager under pressure.

"I'd rather switch him and Delaney, give Williams a day to rest. If Delaney screws up, I can use the two new guys as closers." He stopped pacing and leaned over her desk. "So, how are we doing with him, Ms. Megan? Is his head on any straighter?"

Before she could reply, Brian's voice came from the doorway.

"Why don't you just ask the man in question?"

Dave pivoted. "Because I already did. And you gave me a girlie answer. 'I'll do my best, Dave.'" The man mimicked a high-pitched woman's voice. "This isn't Little League, Delaney."

Megan covered her mouth. Dave would not appreciate her laughter. But he was so funny. She dared a glance at Brian and looked away quickly. His eyes were the brightest green yet.

"When I was born," said Brian, "the doc was amazed."

"'Cause there were two of you?"

"Nah. He'd delivered twins before, but it was a first when one baby showed up with a baseball in his hand while the other held a bat."

Dave's face turned red. "Bah! Here comes the clown again. Are you planning to juggle again out there on the mound, or pitch a winning game? I'm outta here. Do your job tonight."

He slammed the door behind him, and Megan waited until the reverberation settled. "You enjoyed messing with him, Brian, and that's not fair."

"I give as good as I get. Dave Evans wants to win, but he doesn't believe in me. So I rattle his chain. Seems fair."

She understood his point. If a player didn't feel the support of his manager…his confidence could be easily undermined.

"I thought we covered a lot of ground the other night, Brian. So the bigger question is if *you* believe in you."

"Well now, he drawled, "hanging out your shingle again?"

"No," she said emphatically. "I'm a friend, and I care."

His warm smile sent heat waves at her. "Weren't you listening, Meggie?" he asked. "I was born with a baseball in my hand." He started to leave, but turned back. "In fact, I feel a no-hitter coming on."

A no-hitter! No way. "Good timing," she said, keeping her composure. "It's July 3rd, and fireworks are scheduled tonight after the game. The crowd would love to celebrate a win."

His irresistible grin should have warned her. "Oh, I'm counting on fireworks, Meggie, and I'm definitely planning to celebrate." This time he left, and closed the door quietly behind him.

She dropped back in her chair, exhaling a breath she suddenly realized she'd been holding. Brian changed personas as quickly as fashion models changed clothes. He was again acting like a flirt and tease. Her thoughts filtered backward. The serious Brian lived in his apartment. The light-hearted Brian occupied Minute Maid Park. Fooling around here was simply part of his M. O.

But a no-hitter? Too much pressure on himself. She certainly wasn't going to mention that crazy notion to Dave just as she hadn't shared the personal information she'd learned about Brian two nights ago.

Why had Brian come to her office in the first place? Taking her phone, she texted him. His reply came quickly.

Will you be at the game tonight?
Yes, with Josh and his counselor. I'm working promotions for a while, needed a sitter.
See you afterward?
Can't promise. The boys...
Got it. Enjoy.

She'd probably seen hundreds of home games since starting her position with the Astros, and she'd seen Brian on the mound many times. But today, an unfamiliar frisson of excitement flowed through her in anticipation of that evening. She'd started to know the man, started to understand him as a complete person, and to her surprise, actually liked him. Liked him a lot.

##

Her nephew wouldn't be left behind, so Megan had three boys with her that evening. She wasn't worried. Before they'd gotten into her car, Danny took charge with swift reminders that if the young ones didn't behave or went missing, they'd never be able to go to another game. And…he wouldn't come around for a batting practice with them. An eighteen-year-old certainly wielded clout with kids. She chuckled and relaxed. Her instincts about Josh's camp counselor had been good.

They arrived early, and Megan led the three boys to the box she shared with a dozen other employees who chipped in with her for the season. Soft drinks and snacks included. Danny scanned the place as though memorizing it. "Bathroom?" he asked. Good question. She pointed it out to the three of them, then indicated the iconic replica of a nineteenth century locomotive overhead above the field, that moved and whistled for every home run.

"I hope the train makes loads of trips tonight," said Trevor.

"We all do." She paused to take in the wide view. "Look around, boys," she said. "This is a happy place to be. The fans are in a good mood, and our timing is perfect. The players are warming up."

"That's Cleveland," said Josh. "I'm waiting for our guys."

Megan chuckled. "We treat visitors fairly. Everyone has to warm-up." She turned to leave. "Oh, I almost forgot." She pulled three T-shirts from her tote. "Here you go. It's Brian Delaney night."

"Great," said Danny. "Maybe he'll be hot tonight, knowing everyone's got his shirt."

"I'm sure he'll do his best," said Megan. "He wants to win, too."

"I hope so." The kid frowned, shook his head slowly.

"What do you mean, Danny?"

The boy shrugged. "It's just...me and my friends were talking...

"My friends and I... she automatically corrected.

"Geez, you sound like my mother," said Danny with a sigh. "My friends and I were talking...we always talk about the 'Stros...and we really think Delaney can be great. He's got it all. The speed, the placement, fastball, slider, curveball...man, he can be amazing. And he's a great guy. But he doesn't bring the game home enough." He shrugged. "You just never know."

Her heart sank, knowing he was right. Danny and his peers comprised a significant segment of the hometown crowd. If private conversations went along those lines, it was the same talk all over the city. Not that she was too surprised. Brian was up and down on the mound, but overall, the Astros were holding up well enough as a team. But with all the pitching injuries now...

"Enjoy yourselves and behave. I'm sure you'll have company in five minutes. Josh knows everyone. I'll be back in an hour or so after I help out."

"We'll be fine," said Danny. "And thanks. This is a treat."

She waved and quickly made her way to the promotions office, where cartons of T-shirts should have been unloaded and distributed to each gate.

"Are we good?" she asked her co-worker.

"Almost. All hands are on deck," the woman replied. "But thanks for providing backup, Megan, especially with the last-minute change in shirts. Delaney was supposed to be for tomorrow."

"Surviving around here is about being flexible," said Megan with a laugh. "But I love it. You go do what you need to while I stay here and separate stacks. Sometimes, it's nice to be a regular worker-bee."

The woman waved and ran out the door. Megan hummed while doing the simple tasks, her mind at ease and wandering. She had two families to whom she was devoted—her personal family and her Astros family. Both made her happy most of the time. As for the lonely moments after Josh was in bed...? So be it. Better alone than with another loser.

CHAPTER FIVE

An hour later, she returned to the boys, eager to enjoy the game as a plain old fan. She was just in time for the first inning with Cleveland at bat. She glanced at the pitcher's mound. Brian stood there, tall and quiet. Glove on his right hand, ball in his left. Her heart picked up speed as she looked at him. *You can do it, Brian. Make them work for every hit.* Her lips moved in unison with her thoughts.

"Mom! Are you praying?" Josh looked at her, his eyes wider than two suns.

And zoom! First pitch.

"Strike!" Umpire's call.

Brian struck out the first batter with only three pitches.

"He must have had a good warmup in the bullpen," Megan muttered, hearing a happy but surprised buzz around her.

She watched the second batter come up to the plate and take a practice swing. Then…zoom! Three strikes in three throws.

The buzz increased. Megan turned to one of the TV screens, hoping for a close-up of Brian. She saw a man at work. No kidding with the crowd. No dancing in place. His serious demeanor reminded her of his manner at home. Today, he'd brought his no-nonsense side to work.

"He's using an array of pitches," she said to no one in particular, "so how does he know which specific one to use?"

"He must have studied a gazillion videos," said Danny. "Every batter has favorite pitches and not-favorite types. He's messing with them."

"At least with these two," said Megan.

And then it was three. Three batters out with only nine balls thrown. What was called an "immaculate inning." Not often seen in major league baseball. Everyone in Megan's box was on their feet applauding. Everyone in the entire stadium cheered.

She used her cell phone to research. "Hey folks, Delaney is the twenty-third lefty to pitch an immaculate inning. He's now the ninety-fourth pitcher since Major League Baseball began to achieve this. That's over one hundred years."

She began to text him but paused. *Don't rock the boat. Stay away.*

Her phone signaled a text. Scott Cohen. *We didn't ask for miracles, but Harold says thanks.*

Oh my God! She'd almost forgotten about the general manager and team owner. Since meeting Brian, she'd been enjoying their get-togethers. If it wasn't for Dave's constant check-ins, she'd think Brian and she were simply friends.

He struck out the three batters in the second and third innings. Not with only nine pitches, but very close.

Megan kept her eyes on the screen for the better closeup. He seemed to be in his own world. Eyes measuring the strike zone. Eyes on his catcher. Eyes on the batter. Thinking, making decisions. He was inside his own head. She knew the game, knew the concentration it took to do the job.

Her fists clenched in her lap; her stomach flip-flopped with nerves.

I feel a no-hitter coming on.

She froze as his parting words from that afternoon came to mind. In the excitement of his performance, she'd almost forgotten them. What pressure to put on himself. It did make up for all the times he'd fooled around.

He walked a batter to first in the fourth inning, but struck out the two who came afterwards.

In the box she shared with her friends that evening, the team's at-bat times were when they relaxed, which was all backwards, according to Carla.

"Usually we're anxious about getting hits," said Dave's office manager. "Now we're anxious about Delaney's game—in a good way." The woman peered at her. "You had something to do with this" —she waved at the field—"this change in him. Didn't you?"

"Nothing much," Megan replied. "Just talked to him."

"Now you'll be known as the team's whisperer," someone else joked. "Better watch out or there'll be a lineup at your door."

She chuckled with the rest and watched Brian retake the mound. After opening the sliding glass wall to the outdoor seating, she took a seat at the end of a row, curious about the atmosphere in the stadium. Definitely a mixed aura. Quiet-ish. A bit tense. Curious? Confused?

Her fingers twisted against each other. She wanted to watch him live. And alone. But Josh came out and sat next to her. Then Trevor, then Danny.

"Shh... we're not going to talk."

The man was on fire. He struck out the six at-bats in the fifth and sixth inning. Walked a guy in the seventh.

Her stomach rolled. Perspiration dotted her skin. Grabbing her phone, she texted Dave Evans.

How is he?
Quiet. Alone. I'm taking my cues from him.
I'd do the same.
Good. See ya later. Press box.

Later. Right. She turned to the boys. "After the game, you stick with me like glue. We're going to the press box. Don't get lost!"

Danny got quiet, then looked at her. "Ms. Ross, this is the best night of baseball I've ever had in my whole life. No matter what happens with Delaney in the next two innings. Like you said before, when you walk into a stadium, you're in a happy place."

She patted his shoulder. "For a few hours, yes. Yes, you are. And I'm glad you're with us, Dan. Couldn't have pulled this off without you."

A lopsided grin was her reward.

This was the game she loved. It provided all the drama anyone could wish for—from the safety of their seats—and also provided the escape from real worries. During her marriage, she sighed in relief as soon as she entered the gates, leaving her troubles outside them. It was like stepping into Emerald City, where she could forget for a while. Until she couldn't, and filed for divorce and custody. She'd deserved better, and she'd set about getting her own brass ring.

##

The longer Brian pitched, the quieter the crowd became. Stirring. Buzzing. But no roaring. Ticket sales for his next pitched game would be through the roof.

Her text signal came at the top of the ninth. Dave Evans.

Change plan. Dugout. Immediately after. No matter what.

I have three boys with me.

Bring them.

Maybe Cleveland felt spooked by this time. Maybe Brian was so totally in the zone that nothing short of an atom bomb could have stopped him. He brought the game to a close with a perfect ninth inning, and for the first time in her life Megan experienced the meaning of "and the crowd roared."

Brian's teammates ran to the mound, lifted him to their shoulders. Announcers' voices were calling stats. The Astros had won the game with three runs along the way, so it was a win-win all around.

"Let's go, boys."

"Wait, Mom. They're all running the bases, following Brian."

True enough. "I'm on the job, kiddo."

"But there's gonna be fireworks!" said Josh.

"You can see fireworks another time," said Danny. "You don't always get to see the whole Astros team in the locker room."

And that was the difference between eighteen years old and eight years old, thought Megan, glad the teen was with them. He'd be in town for the summer before leaving for college, and she'd take what she could get. Male role models were important.

"Change in plans. How does the dugout sound? Now, will you come?"

Megan led her small troop downstairs to the employees-only area and around to the player doorways. She waved to the security guards, headed inside, surprised to see members of the press gathering, too.

Her eyes sought Brian, but Dave called her. She hustled the boys and went over.

"He hasn't said a meaningful word yet. Just thanked everyone on the team."

"That is meaningful, Dave. What are you expecting?"

"Motivation! I want to know what happened tonight."

"Oh, give me a break! You want me to question a no-hitter?"

The man broke into a grin. "Hey. I'm grateful. I'm not asking him anything. But it's a dang mystery to me."

"That kind of performance is a mystery to everyone. Maybe even to the player," she said.

"Then why don't you ask him?"

She wished Dave would give it up, but he probably wouldn't. "I'm not usurping the role of the press. I work with them, too. And I want them on my side."

She glanced into the dugout again. A pair of green eyes met hers. A smile grew across his face, and he stood up and motioned her over. When they were nose-to-nose with only the fence between them, he said, "Thanks, Meggie. You reminded me why I love this game."

She heard the click of cameras, glad their conversations had somehow helped him. And wished she knew what to do next.

Boom! Boom. Boom. Problem solved. The fireworks were going off and Josh would be happy. But not as happy as Brian. The man was laughing and pointing. "Now that's the way to celebrate!"

"That's what I said too," came Josh's voice next to her. "I love fireworks."

"Joshua Ross!" said Brian, squatting to be more on level with the boy. "Long time, no see. I'm really glad you made it today. You must have brought me luck."

Josh beamed as though the sun shone just for him. Megan groaned softly as she imagined the disappointments ahead. No personal attachments at this point. If at all.

Reporters started throwing questions. Brian straightened up again. "Let's take this inside. See you in the locker room." He turned back to Megan. "You and the boys, too."

Oh, Lordy. The kids had stars in their eyes, even Danny. She couldn't say no, and besides, she was still on the job.

She stayed in the back of the group—the players, reporters, managers, trainers. The door opened once more, and Harold Weber walked in, hand outstretched and a huge grin on his face.

"An amazing performance," he said, shaking Brian's hand. "For you and the team. Congratulations." Cameras clicked, and he waved at the press. "Have at it," he said before stepping back and leaving Brian in the spotlight.

Questions flew all at once until Brian laughed and held up his hands. "Why don't I just tell you the story and then you can ask technical stuff."

"I brought him luck!" Josh's voice came from the front of the crowd.

"Josh!" Megan called, "get back here." She wanted to magically disappear. How had her son wiggled through? And when? She turned to Danny, who shrugged his shoulders, but frankly, didn't look at all put out.

"You sure did," said Brian. "You and your mom."

Would the floor just please open up and swallow her?

"My mom? I don't think she even likes you."

Laughter, guffaws, titters—the sound filled the locker room, and heat rose to her face. Blondes couldn't hide the rosy hues caused by embarrassment. She must have looked like a tomato. "Joshua Patrick Ross! Get over here right now!"

But Brian was laughing along, and shook his head. "Let him stay. He's building a memory."

With those words, all the mad inside her slowly disappeared, and she nodded, knowing he referred to his own life.

He looked out at the group but addressed the reporters. "If you want the story behind the story, it's simple. I had a dad who played catch with me in the backyard. Whether you're a skilled youngster or not, nothing beats having a dad who believes in you. In recent years, I'd forgotten that. So this game is dedicated to the memory of Robert Delaney." He held up his container of sports drink in a toast to his dad.

"Are you saying the psychological prep is more important than the technical skills prep?" asked a reporter.

Megan glanced at Rick, the pitching coach, Dr. Blazer, the sports psychologist, as well as Dave Evans. They were in lockstep, all totally focused on Brian's answer, all seemingly holding their collective breaths.

"That is an excellent question," said Brian slowly. "For a day like today—for me—it had to be both." He pointed at Rick Martinelli. "That man goes the extra mile. I asked him for videos of the Cleveland starting roster just this morning, and I had them all within minutes."

"You studied all those guys just this morning?" asked another reporter. "That's unbelievable."

Brian shrugged and looked uncomfortable. "Uhh…my brother and I have very good memories. My sisters, too, come to think of it. And besides, I've actually pitched against most of those guys over the last few years. So it's no big deal."

Did he mean a photographic memory? If so, that was a very big deal. He'd memorized the strengths and weakness of each opposing hitter and threw the worst pitch each one could hit.

"In theory, a nice formula. In reality, difficult to execute." The press continued its questioning.

"But not impossible," said Brian. "I've felt a no-hitter coming on since early this morning." He found Megan in the back of the crowd. "Remember?"

She nodded. "That's what you said in my office. And I don't understand all this either." She turned to the shrink. "Do you?"

"I can help untangle emotional knots," Dr. Blazer began, "and I can help players achieve potential to be the best they can be. But—" he paused "—I cannot imbue them with talent they don't naturally have."

The place went quiet for a moment. Then more technical questions peppered the air about the hitters, his warmups, his arm now.

Brian stood, moved his arm back and forth. "I'm needing a massage, and that's the truth."

Megan gathered the boys, just as a staff member brought Brian a phone. "It's your brother. Call came through the office. You're not answering your cell." The man smiled. "As if."

"Mom," Josh whispered. "That's Andy Delaney from the Red Sox. Brian's brother is Andy Delaney!"

"I know, honey. Let's give them some privacy."

"But everyone else is still here," he protested.

Sighing, she had to admit he was right.

"Hey, guys," said Brian. "Andy just wanted to remind me that I could never throw a no-hitter to him." His eyes gleamed, his smile reached from ear to ear. "And I wouldn't even try it. Okay, bro. Talk to you later."

He looked out over the small crowd and called it a day. "Thanks everyone. Appreciate your support, but right now, this arm needs a little attention. There's still a full half-season to go! So, let's hear it for our favorite game!

Take me out to the ballgame...Take me out with the crowd," he began.

A beautiful tenor filled the air. She was stunned. How many other hidden talents did the guy have? But she didn't have time to muse. An enthusiastic chorus had joined him.

She gathered the boys, waved to Brian and left the stadium. She needed her own space. One revelation had followed another during a very short time, and her mind was too filled with Brian Delaney. She'd been more comfortable with the stereotype she'd had of him a month ago than with the real man.

CHAPTER SIX

She dropped Danny off before heading home with the two younger boys. It was late, as she'd known it would be, and had arranged a sleepover for her nephew. After bedtime ablutions, she went into Josh's room, where the boys shared the full-size bed.

"Thanks, Auntie Megan. This was the best night ever." Trevor approached her and offered a hug.

"Wow," Megan said. "Now I know you really mean it," she replied, returning his hug in full measure. "Love you, Trevor."

"Don't you think Brian is the best ever person?" asked Josh. "We brought him luck, and he likes us. We should have him over for a cookout." Her beautiful boy beamed at her, then looked at his cousin. "Wouldn't that be cool? And your mom and dad could come over and meet him, too."

Trevor looked at the younger boy and sighed. "Josh, you get some crazy ideas sometimes. Brian Delaney has a big life of his own. He doesn't want to come here when he could be out with his friends. C'mon, I'm tired. We'll throw a ball tomorrow."

"But...but he said I brought him luck! Maybe he'll want more luck." Josh climbed into bed and looked at Megan. "He said so, didn't he? And he said you did, too."

If she were a fairy godmother, she'd grant every wish her son had. Unfortunately, she was simply a mother. "Today was special, Josh. No-hitters don't often happen. Don't you think he's practiced all his life to acquire the skills he needed for such a standout day?"

"Yeah. But...

She couldn't let him go to bed sad. "Maybe, just maybe, a wee bit of our luck kept him company today." She pressed her thumb and pointer finger together and then separated them by a hair. "But just a smidgen. He worked hard and earned it."

"Dad says that's the way it works, too," said Trevor. "You gotta work for something you want."

Her brother and his son. Trevor's words sounded very much like his dad's. Actually, he sounded like her, too! Seemed her irresponsible father had left a mark on both his children to become the very opposite of him.

She kissed them goodnight and retraced her steps to the kitchen. After putting up a tea kettle of water, she allowed her gaze to drift around her home. The nest she had worked and saved for from scratch, the nest she'd created for herself and Josh. Not glamorous like Brian's apartment, but homespun and comfortable. A place where she felt safe. With her mom and Craig as well as her brother's family nearby, she felt connected. Choosing this neighborhood had been a responsible adult decision despite it being a drive to work.

She poured herself a cup of tea and turned on the local nightly news. Almost ten-twenty, just in time for the sports portion.

There was Brian in the dugout, his teammates...and oh, man, Josh and she were standing at the fence! The voiceover commentary faded into the background as she studied Brian's face. Totally relaxed and happy.

The dedication he made to his dad had meant something. And now maybe her task was over, regardless of what he wanted. She wasn't there to feed his ego! Her aim had been to keep him focused. Job done.

The television announcer changed locations. "The celebration is continuing for Brian Delaney at *The Gin Joint.* He won't be on the mound tomorrow, so who can blame him?" The screen shot included Brian and a half-dozen players with wives, girlfriends or singles they'd picked up.

Didn't take long, did it, Brian What happened to the massage he'd needed? Her job was definitely over. She turned off the TV and headed toward her own bedroom, then made a U-turn back to search for her cell phone. Not on the table, but in the bottom of her purse.

A half dozen texts waited.

Did you get home okay?
Call me.
Can you meet us at The Gin Joint?

Oh, pu-leez. The guy, who seemed to like kids, had absolutely no clue about parental responsibility. At times, he acted more like a kid himself. Too similar to her ex. Not only had she'd found her husband gambling with their earnings, but while Megan was pregnant, Lee had acquired a girlfriend. Megan had discovered the affair when Josh was six months old. She'd thrown him out then and there and started over with nothing.

She'd fallen for a guy like her dad. Stupid! She'd learned the hard way, but she'd learned. Despite warming up to Brian, warning lights flashed when she was with him. She plugged the phone in to recharge and went to sleep, needing to recharge herself.

##

A leisurely weekend. She'd taken time off for the July 4th holiday, so the whole family could be together at her mom's place. With everyone supplying food, the simple barbeque would remain simple. In her kitchen, Megan kept one ear attuned to the boys outside, already playing catch, and hummed as she prepared potato salad and coleslaw—her contributions to the meal. For the first time all week, her thoughts wandered everywhere — to books, family, food — except to the team.

Until her phone rang.

Brian. Well, she'd been expecting him to reach out today. Probably didn't understand why she didn't show up last night. She wiped her hands with a dishtowel and connected.

"Hey, Brian. Still flying high from the game?"

"So-so. That was yesterday. Missed you last night."

"I'm not single and carefree, but from what I saw, you managed to have a good time anyway. Which I'm happy about."

"Next time, we'll take Josh and we'll all celebrate."

"To The Gin Joint?" The man lacked all good sense. "Are you kidding me?"

"Of course not! We'll take him...hmm... how about batting cages? There must be some public batting cages we can visit."

There were many places, and it would be fun, but definitely a bad idea. On the list of bad ideas, muddying the waters between work life and private life would be second only to getting involved with the wrong man—again. Time to back away.

"I'm afraid that's not a good plan, Brian, for either of us. You're a nice guy, but you're on your way to making history in the sport. Why don't you just concentrate on that?"

She could have heard the proverbial pin drop in the silence that followed.

"If that's what you want," he said slowly. "Message received. I'll tell Dave you're off the job and save you the trouble. I hope the overtime you earned with this 'nice guy' was worth it." He disconnected.

Megan stared at the phone in her hand. What had just happened? Why did her heart feel heavy? From happily slicing potatoes to being sliced through with grief. Or at least regret. Couldn't two people just have a working relationship? Just be friends?

Sighing with frustration, she now mixed the coleslaw to within an inch of its life. She'd think about Brian later. No black cloud would darken her day with the family. Josh, especially, needed fun time with his mom.

By four that afternoon, she wanted to stuff her ears. Josh and Trevor reveled in reciting all their experiences at yesterday's game, including the dugout and the locker room. She had to bite her tongue to prevent herself from being an ogre.

After getting out of the pool, she flopped on a lounge chair next to Patrick and closed her eyes. Even in the shade, the day was warm, and it was easy to fall into a light doze.

"The boys haven't stopped talking," said Patrick, "but I've noticed that you're being quiet."

She opened one eye. "Nothing left to say, big brother. A day that was different from the rest. And it's over."

"I don't think so." said Patrick.

"You think he's going to hit another no-hitter this season? C'mon. That's a real stretch." Megan chuckled. "Even with the best psychologist in the world… Fuhgeddaboutit."

"I'm not talking about his performance on the field," Pat replied.

"What my husband is trying to say," came the female voice on the far side of Pat, "is that Brian Delaney's eyes were on you the whole time during the interviews. And your brother wants to know what's going on. If anything."

"Nancy! My way is better," protested Patrick.

Nancy swung her legs over the side of the lounge and sat up. "No. If it's something important, just ask."

"You guys could star in your own play. *To ask or not to ask, that is the question….*" Megan paraphrased from the Bard. "Relax. Not interested."

"Liar," Pat whispered.

"Um….," said Nance, peering at Megan. "The color of your cheeks is giving you away."

"He's another drifter," Megan whispered. "A charmer. Everything's a game to him. Not just baseball." A tear leaked from the outside corner of her eye, shocking her. "Dammit."

Her brother's eyebrows rose, and a soft, slow "uh-oh" escaped his lips.

"And I will not take a chance with Josh. Absolutely not. He used to get excited every time I went out with someone new, which wasn't too often. But still—it's why I don't date anymore. Work and family are enough. And I'm very glad he has you, Patrick. I really am."

"Josh is a great kid, and I love him. But I also love you, Meggie, and this is what I know: you're twenty-nine years old with a loving heart. Not dating is not normal."

"It's normal enough for now," she replied.

Nancy rose and waved at Meg's mom. "If you invite him here, we can vet him. Pat would love that."

Megan began to protest, but Nancy held up her hand in a stop motion.

"I saw how he looked at you on television—on our very big screen—despite the hordes around him. His eyes sparkled and he couldn't stop smiling. I don't think it was only because of the no-hitter. You must mean something to him. And now I'm done." She waved her fingers and left to help Kathy and Craig set out the food.

"I love your wife, Pat, but I'm not loving her ideas," said Megan.

"Nancy has great instincts, though. She amazes me over and over again. Just something to think about." He got up and joined Nancy and his parents.

Megan climbed back into the pool. She swam lap after lap—breaststroke, backstroke until finally, she thought she'd gotten Brian out of her system.

##

Brian flew to San Diego with the team on Monday. Maybe getting away would be good for him. No temptation to stop by Megan's office and...and do what? Say what? He had much to say, actually, but he'd begun to learn that words didn't cut it for Megan. She trusted no one and needed proof about everything.

Focus on his career, she'd said. Sure, he could do that. The no-hitter had been a blast, but more than that, his teammates truly celebrated not only for the team but for him. Whatever happened in the future, no one could take that accomplishment away. The calls from Andy and the rest of the Delaney gang — Lisa and Mike, who'd raised him, Jennifer and Doug and even Emily. He chuckled as he recalled that conversation. Someone at Tanglewood had told her about the game, and she'd reported that conversation to her brother.

"If it's a big deal," she'd said, "I'd better call him. We Delaneys are in each others' corners."

And she had called him with all the excitement a person could ask for while bluffing her way through the actual event.

"You know what, Em?" he said with a chuckle, "I'll bet dollars to donuts that you have no clue about what actually happened on that ball field."

"Um... guilty as charged. But I'm so proud of you anyway. Even the nerds up here were talking about it."

He could just imagine.

"Next time, Em, Andy and I will give you a crash course in baseball."

"I love you, bro."

And that's all it took to turn him to mush. Emily, at twenty-six, was so accomplished, yet still so open with her feelings. Innocent. Like a kid. Or maybe just with the family.

"I love you, too, Emily," he'd replied. "Be happy."

He hung up and wondered what had made him end the conversation with those two words. Hmm. She hadn't sounded unhappy. Something inside him was off.

From his seat in the San Diego dugout Monday night, he watched the game, memorizing SD's hitters' stances at bat. What they swung at. Which balls they missed. He was scheduled to start two nights later. He'd chat with that night's pitcher later and talk to Rick. Might as well do it right. Yup, he had a new motto now. *Work hard, play hard. Make his folks proud.* But that was no reason to give up a social life. Even groupies could be fun—maybe later that night, at the hotel bar.

At ten that evening, half the team joined him at the bar; the other half was recovering from the game or preparing for the next day. As for the women...he recognized a couple. Loyal Houston fans. Amazing that they could follow the team so easily.

Within minutes, three women approached his table. "Hey, guys. And hello, Brian Delaney."

"We sure know who the real star of the show is," said Jeff Klein, his favorite catcher.

"Cut it out," said Brian. "Couldn't do it without you. You're the best."

"Hey, I'm not complaining."

Someone else waved the women closer. "Good to see you ladies."

Déjà vu. Brian had been in the same situation hundreds of times. Hotel bars, pretty women, baseball pals—some married, some single—all partying in some way. Poker games were popular, too. Whether it was because of Megan or the recent connection with his family, on this night, he looked around the hotel as though he were hovering over the scene, looking on. Like a sociologist studying group behavior and taking notes.

Brian could have contributed the study's conclusion. Some men were simply enjoying themselves, but most of them were running out the clock until the next game. They were on the road. It was part of their job. Some loved it, some didn't. In the end, the second group just wanted to play ball and return home again.

They were the lucky ones.

He'd begun to hope for some of that luck recently after he'd gotten to know Megan, but obviously, he'd gone wrong somewhere. Women! With three sisters, he should have understood the female dynamic by now. Maybe he'd never paid enough attention.

Megan had been good at winning him over, even though it was just a set-up on behalf of the team. He'd never forget that little meeting in Dave's office. But he and Megan had started to enjoy each others' company, to share ideas. He'd hoped for more, but that last conversation on the phone had definitely set him straight. Like a slap in the face. A betrayal.

Didn't she realize her own fears could prevent her from getting the one thing she wanted most in the world?

A happy life for Josh.

"Hey, Delaney!"

Brian blinked to see Rick coming toward him. "Join the party, Rick. Have a drink."

The coach sat and ordered a beer. Then he leaned closer and spoke softly. "Do you want videos?"

Brian thought about it. "I've got a handle on those who played today. But…it can't hurt."

"Okay… I'll have them for you tonight."

"Is Jeff catching for me on Wednesday?"

"You bet."

"Then let's have a catch tomorrow."

He sat back and raised his glass. "To the beautiful ladies of baseball—may they be fearless, never disappointed, and happy."

Too bad Megan wasn't there to hear him. No matter what, he couldn't wish her ill.

CHAPTER SEVEN

Megan resumed her work without expecting interruptions and didn't have many. She booked many personal appearances for individual team members, mostly with children. Boys and Girls Clubs, hospitals, youth organizations. She arranged future special days for Methodist Hospital as well as a Sunshine Kids party later in the summer. She followed the team's progress as best she could, either in real time television or through replays. Brian had done well, allowing just two hits and one walk. She'd watched every pitch.

Maybe he was taking her advice and sticking to his career. Somehow, the thought didn't cheer her up as it should have.

Dave breezed in on Friday morning. "What's this garbage about you not keeping to our deal?"

"And good morning to you, too," she said. "I'm forfeiting the 'get' money. As you can see, he's on his way. My part's over."

"Oh, no. Not so fast. Your part's over when the season's over. I'm not taking any chances." He paced in a circle, then looked at her, his expression softening. "You did great, Megan. You did wonders. What do they call it? An attitude adjustment. That's what you did for him."

"He did it himself. I just listened."

"Not buying it." He paused a moment. "We've got a three-game series with Boston starting tonight." He eyed her. "Get it?"

The coin dropped. "He's pitching against his brother?"

"Not 'til Sunday afternoon. If his arm's ready."

She thought a moment. "It shouldn't be a big deal. They've been on opposing sides for the last three or four years, right?"

"That was the old Brian. The comedian Brian."

The one who buries his fears.

"This time will be different," continued Dave.

Maybe and maybe not. All she said was, "We'll see."

"As far as I'm concerned, you're still on the job. It's the best thing for the team, and Harold Weber is thrilled with what he sees. So, Megan, please..."

She liked his "please," a rarity from him. Her desk phone rang. She glanced down to see Brian's number. "Speaking of the devil." She picked it up. "Megan Ross."

"Can you contact the Youth Baseball organization we have and tell them that Andy and Brian Delaney will be happy to do some coaching tomorrow morning? I'm pretty sure this arrangement is in your wheelhouse...and you don't have to be personally concerned. There's no Josh Ross listed there. I checked."

Oh, God. "I-I'll let you know."

"What's going on?" asked Dave after she'd disconnected.

"Nothing much—other than he hates me."

Now Dave smiled. "That man does not hate pretty women. Go bark up another tree."

##

Having Andy in town—what a treat! Every season when the team's schedule came out, Brian highlighted the series with Boston. A mini family reunion. Good for his soul. He'd picked Andy up at his hotel and off they went to mentor some kids who needed it. Megan had done her job. A professional through and through. A good cover.

The kids he and Andy worked with on Saturday morning were as excited as they were focused. Their coaches paid attention, too. Pitching and hitting, throwing the ball correctly in the field—contained a lot of nuances and required plenty of practice. They answered a million questions as the kids tried so hard to do it right. The morning passed in a minute for Brian. Before he and Andy left, they passed out the Astros' monthly magazine to each player and posed for dozens of pictures. Smart phones were everywhere.

"Next year, I'll bring Red Sox stuff," teased Andy before the men walked back to Brian's SUV.

"Those kids," said Brian.

"...could've been us," finished Andy.

"Bingo." He waited a moment. "Do you ever think much about what happened back then?"

His brother looked at him with concern. "Of course, I do, But I don't dwell on the past. It's too hard." Andy paused for a moment. "But now that you mention it," he said softly, "I still have Dad's sweater. Remember…?"

"Yup," said Brian. "We wrapped ourselves up in it at night because…"

"…we could still smell him in the wool."

They were both quiet until Brian spoke. "Now, that's a killer memory." He raised the hatchback to stow their gloves and bats, then turned his head to see Andrew. "I'm glad we had each other."

"Me, too, bro. Very glad."

It wasn't until Brian started to drive that Andy began to dig for more. "You're not usually so introspective, Bri. Is anything going on?"

"Are you saying I'm a shallow person?" Which would confirm the general opinion of management.

"You? Absolutely not," protested Andy. "You've got a heart as big as Texas. Wow. Where did that stupid idea come from?" He tapped his fingers on his thigh for a moment. "There must be a woman involved. Women use the word shallow."

Brian's forehead wrinkled, and he started to laugh. Didn't know why but it felt darn good. "Thanks for that. You are the best medicine."

His brother's smile grew and soon a chorus of laughter filled the car.

"Unfortunately," said Brian, "the woman in question thinks I'm a loser like her dad. Thinks I've lost too many games I could have won. Won't let me near her kid. Doesn't want attachments. Her last words to me were, 'focus on your career.'"

"Ouch."

"Exactly."

"So when can I meet her?" Andy asked. "I'll straighten out her thinking in no time."

"Thanks for the offer, but this is one problem I have to figure out by myself. I'm not even sure she's at the office this weekend. I'm glad you have my back, though."

"Count on it. You and I? We were born our own team."

"Except on the diamond recently," Brian mused. "That's the only place a game between us is played to win."

"And that's the truth."

Just as they pulled into Minute Maid Park, Brian's cell rang. His eyebrows lifted when he saw the name of the caller. "What can I do for you, Ms. Ross?"

Andy pointed at the displayed call, his head tilted in inquiry.

Brian nodded.

"How did the morning go?" she asked.

He maneuvered into his spot, moved his seat back so he could stretch his legs and be comfortable for this conversation. "We made them cry, Megan," he replied. "That's what Delaneys do. We make kids cry. And then we leave. Just ask Andy. He's still with me."

Silence at the other end. A rather painful one at that.

Brian sighed. "Just kidding, Megan. It was great. Half the time they couldn't tell Andy from me until they confirmed our playing arms. My brother's right-handed. I'm sure you'll check it out with the coaches."

"It's-it's my job, Brian. I'm another layer of protection for the team and the children."

"Point taken. Is that all you need? We're on our way into the locker room."

"There's something else…I have some bad news."

He felt himself tense. His stomach knotted as a variety of thoughts raced through his mind. "Is it business or...was Josh hurt? Where is he? How bad?"

"No, no, no. Josh is fine. I'm fine. No one's sick."

He laid his head against the seatback and caught his breath. *Idiot.* She wouldn't be as calm if her son was in trouble. "Then there's no bad news," he said quietly. "Everything else can be resolved."

"I'm not sure I agree," Megan said, "but I'm very sorry if I scared you. Let's just say, I have news you won't like."

"Spill it."

"Do you have time to come up to my office now? I'll be here for a few more minutes before meeting up with Josh at my mom's."

He glanced at his quiet brother. Andy gave him a thumbs up.

"I'm on my way."

##

He pointed Andy to the locker rooms and clubhouse. "Grab some lunch, and maybe I'll find you later. I'm not in the lineup tonight."

"No problems, bro. I'm sure some of my tribe is inside. Good luck upstairs."

She was on another call, so Brian stood in the doorway, drinking her in. So pretty in that all-American way. Blonde hair gathered into ponytail, bangs across her forehead, and gold loops shining in each ear. She looked up, flashed a quick smile and waved him in as she hung up the phone. "Would you close the door behind you, please?"

"Sure."

When their privacy was assured, she stood and walked around the desk, waved him to a chair and sat down near him.

"You don't like talking across a desk," he said. "I've noticed that." As well as many other traits which he'd refrain from discussing.

"Let's just say for starters that you're not 'business as usual' and, second, I'm not your supervisor." Her hands sat in her lap, fingers interlacing and twisting around each other. He'd seen that before.

"You said you had something to tell me," he prodded.

"Yes, and you're not going to like it."

He couldn't imagine anything he wouldn't like if it involved her. "Time's a-wasting, Meg. Just come out with it."

"We're working together again," she said quickly. "It comes from the top. The very top. For the rest of the season." She could barely meet his eyes.

She was so uneasy…something was bothering her, something besides the work situation. Well, turnabout was fair play, and two could play the psychology game. Maybe he'd be doing her a favor.

"And how do you feel about that, Megan?" he asked quietly.

She raised her eyes to him. "Partnering with you again is not really bothering me, Brian. You are really good at what you do—when you want to be. I admire serious effort. But we need to clear up something first," she said. "At least I do." She inhaled and sighed a big sigh.

"I'm listening," he said, keeping his voice low.

"I want to apologize for that last phone call we had—the 'you're a nice guy but jump in a lake' speech. It's one of my usual send-offs, but you didn't deserve it. I was pretty brutal, and I'm sorry." Her eyes met his then, and he saw the remorse, the normally bright blue now dark and shadowed. He wanted nothing more than to kiss those shadows away. Instead, he forced himself to sit still.

"If it makes you feel better," she continued, "I had a crappy day afterwards. I killed the coleslaw and swam until I couldn't breathe."

Now they were getting somewhere. "Apology accepted, Megan, and no more *mea culpas.*" He leaned back and stretched his legs out. "Did I ever mention that my family is comprised of strong, confident women? You'd fit—uh, you're just like them." Didn't want to scare her.

"Thanks for the compliment," she said. "I know your family means the world to you."

"That's the truth."

"I'm in your corner, Brian, but I'm not your sister. This is a business relationship—the game, events—I'm your career support, and nothing else. That rule hasn't changed. Are you okay with that?"

Other than the fact that he didn't need anyone to lean on, he was fine. But what was wrong with doing his job and exploring their relationship? He wasn't going to rock Megan's boat, however, at least not yet. Spending time with her sounded promising. The apology she gave him made her a stand-up person.

"You can write a million rules books, Megan, but in the end, people are human. That's what I know."

##

DELANEY TWINS FACE EACH OTHER AT
MINUTE MAID
SOLD OUT GAME
Dateline: Monday, July 13

*What happens when a talented pitcher faces an
elite batter and they're both named Delaney? Fans get a
baseball game to remember! Yesterday afternoon,
Houston squeaked out a 2-1 win, but it could have easily
gone the other way.*

*A strikeout against Andy Delaney in the second
inning had Astros fans dancing. Would their inconsistent
pitcher hold it together all the way through? Brian
Delaney— you love him or hate him. Then love him
again. Coming off a no-hitter game two weeks ago, the
crowd had high expectations, but held its collective
breath through the next confrontation of brothers, which
ended in a walk.*

*If third time's a charm, then Brian's luck held in
the sixth inning when he struck out his brother for the
second time in the game.*

*By the top of the ninth, the Stros were up 2-0 when
power hitter Andy Delaney came to the plate for the
fourth time—and a different ending. Slam! Into the
crowd. He strolled around the bases. Score 2-1. But
that's the way it remained when brother Brian showed
his stuff and struck out the next two batters to end the
game.*

*Whether in front of a crowd or a behind-the-scenes
story, nothing tops baseball at its best.*

##

Megan read the article at her desk the next day and
nodded. Of course, the game required eighteen guys or
more, but the storyline that captured the imagination had
been captured by the sportswriter. Twin brothers. Best
friends. Both in the majors. Facing off against each
other. Then hugging afterwards.

She'd been there, had seen them in action with her
own eyes. They'd each played to win, but the job didn't

supersede family. It said something about them. About Brian. And maybe about her as well. She stood and walked to the window, eyes unfocused. Brian was a good guy, his brother, too. But she…wouldn't let Brian into her world. Such fear. Her brother may have been on to something. It wasn't normal.

Josh had been with her yesterday, expecting to be allowed any place his mom went. Brian had spotted him immediately.

"My good luck charm is back!" He'd high-fived her son outside the locker room and met her gaze. "You doing all right?"

"Me? I'm fine. What about you?"

He'd chuckled. "I'll be taking it easy for a couple of days. Soft tissue work, light throwing, light stretching, visit the weight room. The usual."

"Sounds like a plan. A good one. Especially with All-Star Week starting tomorrow. You're on vacation, so you can really recuperate while the rest of us peons go to work!"

"You sure like that word." He turned to Josh. "Is that all she does? Work?"

"Yup. And take care of me. We swim at Grandma's a lot."

"Josh! That's enough." She'd glanced from her son to Brian, who seemed to be ready to ask more questions. "We're heading home now, but call me in the unlikely event you need anything. Congrats, again, on the game."

She'd rushed out of there without giving Brian a chance to comment about her boring life. Josh needed duct tape across his mouth!

A text had come in afterwards.

Going to Boston with Andy. Different flight. Will meet up with the team in Pittsburgh. Thx.

When she'd read his words, she instantly felt she was babysitting again. No advance planning. Did he even have a plane ticket to Pittsburgh? Was that her responsibility, too? She'd been right to keep her distance from him, after all.

She reached for her phone, ready to rip into him. Then paused and called Dave. Everything checked out. All-Star Week was vacation time and players often went home.

She texted a reply:

Enjoy yourself and the family visit.
Work and family. Just like you. See ya in a week or so. B.

P.S. Try to miss me.

Miss him? She'd been instantly ready to find fault without reason. Why did she still expect the worst in him?

She turned from the window. A peaceful week lay ahead. The kind she liked. The type she'd been used to BB—Before Brian. No drama. No roller-coaster highs and lows and no...excitement... No dancing green eyes in her doorway, no cute smile, no long legs stretched out in her office with the man totally at ease. No occasional "Meggie" floating in the air.

She plopped into her chair and held her head in her hands. What was wrong with her? Being unsettled felt strange. She'd worked hard to keep her orderly life together.

Was it loneliness? She could call one of her friends and go pubbing, plan a beach day in Galveston or some other activity. A pleasant thought, but not one to quell her unease. So, general loneliness was off the list.

Josh? Her son was fine, happy. No family worries. All good in that department.

Did she actually miss Brian? He'd been gone only a day, but as she pictured his warm smile, those happy gleaming eyes, that confident walk, her breath hitched in her throat. The next week and a half loomed bleak and boring. No racing heart, no surprises...

"Oh, no-o-o...." Her thoughts led to only one place. He'd gotten to her, past all her defenses. She cared about him, cared too much. Once more, she was attracted to the wrong type of guy. Hadn't she learned anything in life? A man with his reputation could be ruinous to both her and Josh. What was she thinking?

Taking a deep breath, she tried to sort fact from fiction. *Fact:* since she'd been working with him, she'd seen almost none of that irreverent behavior except in the beginning. *Fact:* his game performance had greatly improved. *Fact:* He was sexy, cute, and built. He moved with an athletic grace she admired. Lowering her lids, she pictured a pair of gleaming eyes—and they were bright green.

Fiction: Believing she was not attracted to him.

Fact: She was in trouble.

CHAPTER EIGHT

Calls or texts came in every night Brian was away. She started making notes, jotting down questions—all business related. The safer route. Until the last night of the road trip, which had begun in Pittsburgh but had continued to Atlanta. He called from there.

"Miss me?" he asked. Humor laced his voice, but she also sensed a drop of apprehension, or maybe it was hope.

"Hmm...I'll admit it's been somewhat boring around my office."

"I'll take that as a yes."

"Ever the optimist."

"There's no other way, Meggie, if you want a chance at the brass ring. Where would I be now if Lisa and Mike hadn't been optimistic about taking on four kids when they were still kids themselves?"

"Point taken." She knew more of his background now, how his oldest sister dropped out of law school to marry her fiancé, Mike Brennan, a rookie quarterback with the Boston Riders at the time. Ten years later, he held three Superbowl wins.

"Tomorrow's a travel day, Meg. I'll be home early. How about meeting up for dinner?"

"Dinner? You mean like a date?"

His warm chuckle melted her before he spoke. "It has been done before. Man, woman, dinner date. I can pick you up at the office."

"Not the office." Especially on his first day back. Her mind clicked with possibilities. "How about meeting at *La Roma Bella* in the Galleria? And that's only if Josh can go to my mom's tomorrow night."

"I'll make a reservation," said Brian. "Six o'clock?"

"Perfect."

"That's exactly right."

As she hung up, she could still hear his laughter in the background.

One date. She'd give him one date to get him out of her system, to be up close and personal with another charmer and cut him off without regret.

###

Houston's traffic could never be called light, especially through the commuter hours. When Megan finally pulled up to the restaurant, she saw Brian waiting outside, checking his watch, mouth tight. He scanned the area repeatedly as cars entered the lot.

She found a spot and strode toward him, waving, and watched his transformation to a relaxed and smiling man.

"Oh, this was a bad idea," she said as he held the door open for her.

"Already? C'mon, give me a break."

She started to laugh. "Not you. The traffic."

"You just gotta roll with it,"

Laughing again, she said, "Roll? If only it would."

"Well, I haven't lost my touch," he said, as they followed the server to a table in the back. "If I can make Megan Ross laugh twice in five minutes, I'm having a winning streak."

"That's some rep I have," she said, a bit subdued as she was seated.

"Nope," he said. "Everyone loves Megan Ross. You shut down only with me."

"I treat…"

"But here's the thing," he interrupted. "I opened up only with you."

Her chin shot up, and she met his gaze as the truth of his statement sank in.

"Interesting, huh?" he commented, then turned to the server. "Give us some time. There's no rush with the meal."

"Yes, sir, Mr. Delaney."

"Hang on," said Brian with a sigh. He reached for his wallet and whipped out a large bill. "There's no Mr. Delaney here. I am invisible."

The server looked from Brian to the money. "Yes, sir, Mr. Smith."

And they were alone again.

"I-I've only seen that done in the movies," said Megan. "Sometimes I forget you're famous."

"That's exactly the way it should be between us," said Brian, leaning back in his chair.

"There's an us?"

85

A smile began, warm, tender and teasing. "Of course, there's an us. Aren't we here? Aren't we friends? Didn't we miss each other?"

She couldn't afford another mistake, but she couldn't argue any of his points either. Rolling her eyes, she cried, "Uncle. I give up!"

His laughter was contagious. When she caught her breath again, and he reached for her hand, she let it stay within the circle of his.

"Now," he said, "that's better."

"Yes," she said slowly. "For the moment." She met his gaze. "I like you, Brian…"

"But you're cautious. Afraid. I know that. But I also know the way to overcome that fear is to spend time with me. Off the field."

His words made sense, but something still niggled at her. "I'm sure you've met dozens of beautiful women in this city, attended elite parties and events. That's so not my crowd, not my world."

"I know," he said, nodding. "You are head and shoulders above them all. You are a lioness. I've been in Josh's shoes, Megan, and know that he's in good hands."

She melted. He couldn't have paid her a higher compliment. "But this doesn't mean you can go back to fooling around on the job," she said, swallowing hard.

"And have you lose your bonus?" His eyes sparkled as he spoke. "I wouldn't think of it."

She straightened her posture. "I've earned every penny of that bonus. And besides, how did you know about the bonus?"

He winked. "I figured you'd demand one! It's better pay than overtime."

##

The more time she spent with him, the more she liked him. No question. The stories of his siblings, his childhood in Boston...He kept the stories light and carefree, when she knew darkness had shadowed them. Two hours passed in a heartbeat before they walked to her car. She unlocked it and turned toward him.

"I had a good time. I really did."

Brian put his hands above the door and leaned toward her. His lips touched hers lightly, sweetly. Hmm...Nice. Exciting. She rose on tiptoe and that was all the encouragement he needed for his tongue to trace her mouth, then explore in depth. Her eyes closed, and she shivered as the kiss deepened before she broke away.

"Oh, wow...that was a surprise."

His breathing sounded labored. "A good one, I hope?"

"I-I think so." Even to her own ears, she sounded amazed. And Brian's laughter confirmed it.

He leaned forward again and stole a quick kiss. "I may have said it before, Meggie, but there's no one else like you in the world."

"Technically true, but I know what you mean. Thanks, but now I'm embarrassed. So good night!" She grinned up at him and opened the car door.

"All set?" he asked as she snapped her seatbelt closed.

"I'm good to go," she replied. "Will I see you tomorrow?"

In the glow of the parking lot lanterns, she saw his eyes brighten, his smile grow. "Count on it." He pointed his forefinger at her. "I know where you work."

He rapped on her hood in goodbye and walked away. She stared after him for a moment, trying to absorb the aftereffects of the lovely evening. Then, with her hand on the gear shift, she started the car, turning her head and ready to back up, when she heard another rap above her. Rolling down the window, she looked up, expecting Brian.

"Hello, sweet meats. Glad to see me after too long a time?"

Lee! Her stomach twisted, and beads of sweat popped out on her lip. Why was he here? A coincidence? Had he randomly spotted her in the lot?

"No, I'm not. Never wouldn't be long enough." She pressed up on the lever to raise the window, but her ex pushed down on the pane's edge. "If you don't walk away from here," she said, mustering a steady voice, "I'll make some noise." She placed her hand on the horn, ready to press down.

The man shrugged. "No one will care." He put his face closer to hers, and nausea rose in her gut.

"You're hanging around with money now," he said. "It was all over the television. Your picture. Him. I need that money, sweets. A lot. And I need it bad."

Which meant he was gambling. "Work for it." She started backing up slowly, hands shaking on the wheel.

"How's my son?" he asked. "Haven't seen him in a while. Maybe too long…"

Show no fear. Show no fear. "You have no son," she said. "Remember? You gave him up. Now, get away from this car, Lee, because my foot's on the pedal and I'm leaving."

"You don't understand, Ms. Moneybags. If I don't make payment, I'm a dead man." His bloodshot eyes verified the truth of his words.

"Sorry about that, but it's not my problem. Good luck." She shifted to reverse and turned her gaze toward the backup screen.

His hand came into the car and he pushed her head around until she faced him. "Josh is all the luck I need," he said. "The boy means a lot to you…."

She wanted to punch him, pound him. *Don't get out of the car.*

"Try suing for custody, Lee. You'll be laughed out of court."

This time she succeeded in driving off, her mind racing. Until she came to the one conclusion that made sense. Lee didn't want Josh. Never had. He didn't want any kind of custody. He wanted to use Josh for extortion. If she didn't pay, he would...what? Kidnap his own son?

Yes. He certainly would now. When she'd met him, Lee had been a lot of fun, and sharp, with a smile that didn't quit. His eyes had lit up when he looked at her. Until the next shiny thing came along. In retrospect, she realized that their marriage was used as a cover for respectability. As a tool for his non-stop gambling. She'd been clueless back then. Naïve and stupid.

Nothing had changed. In Lee's mind, kidnapping Josh for ransom would solve his money problems. Only to him would that make perfect sense.

##

"No camp for him today," said Megan the next morning when Brian joined her in the doorway to her office, and she'd told him what had happened. Josh had gone to use the men's room, and she was keeping an eye out for him. "I'm going to hire a bodyguard for a few weeks until school starts again. I do not trust that man."

"You should have leaned on the horn last night," he said. "The guy would be mincemeat today and no threat to anyone." He stepped closer and held her around. "You must have been petrified."

"Shocked and frightened...I'll admit. The man is beyond help. And—and I'm afraid for you, too. He might wait outside after a game and follow...maybe we should hire two bodyguards."

His laughter lightened her soul, and she chuckled along. "Here's my little man," she said as Josh ran over, his eyes shining when he saw her visitor.

"I hear you and your mom are taking in the afternoon game today," said Brian.

"Yup. But you're not pitching till Sunday." He turned to Megan. "Can we come back?"

"We'll see."

He wrinkled his nose and appealed to Brian. "That is the worst answer a mom can give a kid. We'll see, we'll see."

"Yeah, that's a tough one," said Brian, "but it's better than a 'no,' isn't it?"

Josh's forehead furrowed. "I guess."

That's the kind of guidance a boy needed from a good man. Not the neglect and disregard he'd gotten from Lee.

"Nice job, Bri," she said quietly.

"I'll go one better," he said. "Josh, how'd you like to join me for lunch today in the clubhouse with the guys?"

As the words sunk in, her son's face radiated happiness. He was over the moon.

"Really?" asked Josh. "With you and-and Jeff Klein, and Travis Watson?"

"And anyone who's having lunch. Today's game is at 3:10, so I'd think the place will be pretty full for a light lunch. Whaddayasay?"

"I say, yes!" He stretched his skinny arm to high-five with Brian.

"Atta boy. Your mom can bring you over."

"But she's not staying, right?"

"It's man time, my friend. You're with me."

This. This is what her son had been missing. Baseball happened to be Brian's career, but positive attention from a good man in any field would have worked. She caught Brian's eye and mouthed, "thank you."

"My pleasure. Bring him about noon. I'll text you."

"Perfect."

"You won't forget, Mr. Delaney, will you?"

"Not a chance. And from now on, you can call me Brian."

And he didn't forget. Megan's phone signaled at 11:45. She read the note, caught Josh's eye. "Ready for lunch?"

"Yup. But I'm not very hungry, so please don't talk about clean plate clubs and all that baby stuff."

She twirled him around. "You are too funny, Josh. And I love you so much."

"I know. So, can we go now? Mr. Brian's waiting."

Five minutes later, they entered the Astros' clubhouse. Brian approached them immediately. While Josh stood looking around, Brian spoke quietly to Megan.

"I've made some phone calls and lined up several interviews for you."

"What?"

He nodded at Josh. "For his protection."

"But I never asked...I'm capable..."

"Slow down and listen. Remember who Mike Brennan is, my brother-in-law, who raised me?"

She nodded.

"Well, don't you think he had some issues protecting us too? Please, Meggie. I'm not stepping on your motherly toes. I'm just helping out. Trust me."

So earnest. Sincere. So serious. This was Brian Delaney who pulled no punches. "God help me," she whispered. "But I think I do trust you."

He paused, and a small smile lit his face. "Josh needs a secure, ordinary life, just like we did back then." Now he actually chuckled, his forehead wrinkling. "An ordinary life—whatever that's supposed to be. Right now, it's baseball camp. Soon it will be school. I've been there, done that. The very same thing."

She glanced at her son, who was still taking it all in. Some of the players were saying hello to him, pausing to chat. Waving to her. So nice of them. Of course, Brian may have put a bug in their collective ear.

"And you, Meggie," the man continued, "you need a normal life too, without worrying about a crazed ex-husband. I've arranged for Security to walk you to your car every night when I'm not available."

"But they can't just…"

"It's on me, Meg. All of it. You interview and hire. I'll pick up the bill. Life's too short, and I'm simply paying it forward." He focused on Josh then. "Hungry?"

"Maybe," he said, cautiously glancing at Megan before responding. "What are you eating, Mr. Brian?"

Megan, the mom, said nothing about food choices. Just watched them walk away, the big man's arm around Josh's shoulders while the boy looked up at him in earnest conversation.

Megan, the woman, wondered if stars shone in her eyes, too. The responsible and mature Brian Delaney she'd gotten to know in the past month did not at all resemble the Brian Delaney who'd juggled baseballs in her office when this experiment had first started. Only occasionally since then, as when he ran the bases with the kids after a home game—the only player to do so— did he resemble that happy-go-lucky fellow.

But a month meant nothing. He could easily slide backward again.

##

They lost on Sunday night, which gave life to Megan's fears. Of course, no team won every game, but Brian was unfocused, certainly couldn't find the strike zone and was taken out in the fourth inning. She couldn't blame Dave Evans one bit for that. Instead of helping Brian, she wondered if their relationship was hurting him. He didn't need the distraction of a close friend with a nasty ex-husband.

She and Josh watched the game from home. When his eyes started to close, she reminded him about Paul, the new counselor he'd have at camp the next day—right along with Danny.

"You'll be sick of baseball by the time summer's over," she teased.

"Mom! No way." Josh roused himself enough to retort. "I'll never be sick of baseball. I hope Paul is good."

She walked her sleepy son to his room and tucked him into bed. And then she simply watched him breathe. Her beautiful boy—who would now be protected by Paul from morning 'til night. Fortunately, the guard knew baseball and looked young enough to pass for a counselor—if a person didn't examine him too closely. Josh and his friends would believe the story. And the camp's administrators had been totally cooperative after examining Paul's credentials.

Brian had come through, making calls and setting up interviews. He really had put words to action. By Friday night, she'd met with three candidates. Arrangements had been solidified on Saturday. Which led her thoughts around to Brian again. He'd been so good to her, especially concerning Josh, but maybe she was not good for him. Maybe she should step back.

A lump formed in her throat at the thought. He'd brought lightness and fun to her. She swallowed hard, but tears threatened, then flowed. She brushed them away. Crying was not her style, but, oh, her heart hurt, as though a corner of it had been ripped away.

The longing took her by surprise. How could he have become so important to her in only a month?

As for his feelings? Well, he had a soft heart and needed a friend. His paying it forward comment could have been applied to anyone in his orbit. But...that smile whenever he spotted her...that certainly was unique to Megan. As were the daily calls, texts or visits.

Impatient with herself, she prepared for bed, too, vowing to speak with Brian the next day.

Her cell rang in the morning at ten.

"Did Paul show up at the campgrounds?"

"Well, good morning, and yes he did, right on time. I think this will work out, Brian. Even Danny's accepted him as another counselor. I'm going to give Danny a big tip at the end of the season. He's been great with Josh."

"That's not too hard, Meg. Josh is a sweet kid. Just like his mom."

"Oh-h. Brian, I wanted to ask you—well, anyway, sorry about last night's game, but as Josh says, 'you can't win them all.'" She sounded like a pre-teen. Ugh.

"He's right."

"I just hope that-that you weren't distracted because of us, you know, Josh and me. Because that wouldn't be good for your career."

She heard only silence on his end for a long moment. "Can we get something out of the way, here, Meggie? I love being distracted by you and Josh. You are not responsible for how I perform on the mound. Only I am. If you had real influence, I'd bet I'd have a no-hitter game every time I played." He paused. "I'm not wrong about that, am I, sweetheart?"

Her breathing hitched. Sweetheart? "No," she whispered. "You're not wrong."

"How about lunch today?" he asked.

She glanced at her business calendar. "Yes," she replied, already looking forward to it. "Make sure to bring your phone so we can schedule in some new events. I want to book you and Jeff into Texas Children's and the Veterans Medical Center when you get back from the next road trip. A pitcher—catcher duo always goes over well. You're both good at visiting all types of patients."

"Yep. Okay. Clubhouse at noon today?"

"First Josh, and now his mother?" she asked.

His hearty laughter set her laughing, too. "But the food's good, Meggie."

"You're absolutely right about that."

"And the company's better."

The company's better. "You might be right again, Brian." She felt herself smile, felt a rush inside. Hadn't had that experience in years. Brian Delaney— caring, protective and sensitive, too. A big heart.

"See you later," she said and disconnected.

She gave herself a moment to daydream, then got to work again. In addition to the medical center visits, she needed to confirm the Astro's wives' charity exhibition game scheduled for a Saturday in mid-August, the 15th, at Minute Maid. Texas Rangers vs. Houston Astros. Women in the afternoon; men in the evening. Megan looked forward to coaching the ladies again this year, her third time. Her record so far was 1-1. She giggled at some awkward memories and shook her head. Not really a competition. Just a fun way to raise money for charity.

The weeks ahead actually showed promise, maybe a new lease on life if…she didn't have to worry about bodyguards, ex-husband threats and risking her heart.

CHAPTER NINE

Brian didn't like road trips anymore. He wasn't enjoying groupies anymore either. The only female who'd ever captured his attention was back in Houston. A three-day series in Tampa followed by three days in Miami seemed like an eternity. One win, one loss for him. He spent whatever downtime he had playing cards with a few of the guys.

Phone calls and texts every single day or night assured him all was well with Josh and his bodyguard, whom Josh had called "cool and a good player." Perfect. Paul had adjusted to a counselor's role well. More important, Megan liked the guy and trusted him.

"But I wish we didn't need him!" she'd said last night on the phone, the day before his return to H-Town.

"Maybe we can cut that need short," he'd said slowly.

"How?"

"So far, Meggie, we've been playing only defense. Maybe it's time to go on offense. Or as Mike would say, an interception is in order."

"You're scaring me, Brian," she said quietly. "What do you mean?"

"I'm going to put a tail on him."

As soon as the words were out of his mouth, he felt better. Less tense about leaving Meg and Josh alone. She'd confided in her family for safety's sake, but they were also part of the defense, like sitting ducks, waiting to be surprised.

"A tail? Like on detective shows…?" she asked, her voice doubtful. "I don't know…that's pretty scary. He might catch on. And I have no idea where he is, where he stays. I know nothing! Which is how I liked it—until now."

"We'll find out. Knowledge is power, sweetie, and I'd much rather act than have to react on the spot."

He heard her chuckle, didn't get the joke. "What? What's so funny?"

"Brian, you're excellent at both."

Maybe she had a point. He'd picked off two base runners in Miami and three in Tampa—such a kick to hear the umpire's "o-u-t!"

"Thanks, Meg, but I'm not always around."

"Point to you. This time, however, send the bill to me. I can't think of a better way to spend the extra I'm earning than on the safety of my son."

And you. "We can talk about it later."

"Bri-an," she warned. "You're doing enough. I'm serious about this."

"And I hear you. We'll talk. How about tomorrow evening? We'll be back by noon. No game. And if you can get off work early, we'll have some extra time."

There was a pause, and he held his breath.

"Would you like to come over for some grilled burgers with Josh and me on my patio?"

The inner sanctum. "That is the best offer I've had in my entire life." As soon as he hung up, he punched the air with a huge "Yes!"

Just like a kid.

##

She'd given him her address and he used Waze to find it. In the four years he'd been in the city, he'd had no reason to wander into family-friendly territory. His single lifestyle led him to clubs, bistros and hot spots that provided action.

Megan's community was neither gated nor guarded. A bit older, with mostly single-level brick, ranch-style homes. Grassy front yards with beds of flowering plants and evergreen bushes bordering the foundations. Lots of orange daylilies greeted him everywhere. It looked like a place to call home.

Her house was on a small cul-de-sac with three others. The Honda sat in the open garage, which should not have been left open. He'd slip that into the conversation later. He pulled into the driveway, gathered the bottles of wine he'd brought and opened the door. Josh joined him immediately, along with his cousin, Trevor.

"Hey, you really came!" said Josh, with a high five.

"Your mom invited me. Nice to see you, too, Trevor."

The boy nodded and mumbled something.

From the corner of his eye, he saw the door open. And there was his prize in a bright blue sleeveless top and shorts. He couldn't stop staring. Oh, yes, he was definitely a leg man.

She waved them inside. "Come on, it's cooler in here." The kids went ahead, but he held back until he and Megan were alone.

"You look great, Meggie. Even better than at work." He stepped closer and brushed a few locks of hair off her neck. He studied her lovely face, leaned down and found her mouth with his. "I've been fantasizing about another kiss."

She relaxed in his arms, her weight resting against him. "But not in the doorway, okay?"

Laughing, he allowed her to pull him inside and handed over the wine. "It's a deal."

She led him down the hall, where on one side he saw a living-dining room combination while on the other side, study or den. A nice-sized kitchen waited at the end. A busy, bustling, kitchen with snacks and drinks and suddenly... voices. The voices in his head that belonged to another house with a similar family feeling. Echoes of Woodhaven, Massachusetts.

His heart lurched as he took it all in. "You did it right, Meg," he said, the sound raspy. "This is a real home. Like when I was a boy."

"Oh, Brian...I am so sorry." She raised her face toward him, stricken, her hand on her heart.

"It's good, Meggie. It's good." Then he intentionally broke the mood. "So who's setting the table, boys?"

"Already done on the patio," said Josh. "And we have lots of fans going."

"Then who wants to play catch for ten minutes?" he asked and got a quick response from both kids.

"I suggest the backyard for privacy," said Megan.

"But, Mom, there's more room on the street. We want to throw far."

"No problem," said Brian. "Consider this a warm-up and skills practice. Backyard it is. I'll get my glove."

"And I'll get mine," said Megan. "I'm not being left out. A good time for everyone."

And it was, even when he stopped the action to give the boys pointers. Megan listened hard too, trying to memorize everything he said.

"Hey, girl. Don't work so hard. I'm not disappearing."

Her smile always got to him. "I'm coaching the wives for next Saturday's game. I figured I could bring something new to tomorrow's practice."

"And I figured there was a reason. Always glad to help out." His stomach rumbled just then. "Did you say something about dinner?"

"I certainly did. Protein, carbs, vitamins and lots of electrolytes."

"Translation, please."

"Hamburgers, potato salad, green salad, corn on the cob. Sports drinks. And—a glass of wine."

"Perfect."

He used that word a lot. But frankly, the evening was perfect. Chatter and laughter, the sounds of happy people. Memories churned again.

"Let's see if the boys and I can get the place spic and span before we finish two choruses of *Take Me Out to the Ball Game.*" He started singing, Josh and Trevor joined in, and by the time the second chorus was done, Megan had a respectably clean kitchen.

"Wow, that's a neat trick," she said. "And you carry a tune beautifully."

"Singing always made clean-ups go faster. And there's more where that came from," said Brian. "Andy and I — well, we were the kings of corny jokes." He grabbed a spoon, gave another one to Josh and held his up like a microphone.

"Why are frogs so happy, Josh?"

"I don't know, Mr. Brian," replied the boy, speaking into his 'microphone.' "Why are they so happy?"

"Because they eat whatever bugs them."

Megan rolled her eyes, but the boys laughed as if it was the best joke they'd ever heard. "I could go on," said Brian, winking at Megan, "but I won't."

"A man of many talents," she said with a grin. "Nice."

"I'm not the only one with talents," he said, glancing at Josh and the house. "You did a good job here, Megan. Nice home."

"Thanks, but I wasn't talented enough to prevent my brother from coming over soon, and I can't guarantee he'll be alone. Just a heads-up." She avoided his gaze, and a flush rose on her neck.

"Let's look at it another way," said Brian. "You've actually seen my brother on the field, and now I'll meet yours up close. Not quite the same, but almost."

Her slow smile reassured him.

Trevor piped up. "Can I use your phone, Auntie Meg? I want to tell Dad to bring his glove." He glanced at Brian. "Then we can have a real catch. Two and two."

"Anything for the cause, Trevor," said Brian, reaching over and squeezing Megan's hand. No brother or father or mother could knock him out of the running. This woman had his name all over her. All he had to do was convince her of it.

##

Two out of three wasn't bad. She loved her job and her personal life was getting better and better. But the third leg ruined the other two. Waiting for Lee to make a move—or not—provided a black cloud that hovered no matter how complex her activities. She didn't know whether they'd succeed in keeping track of her ex before or if he acted again. She could provide no ideas about where he hung out—maybe gaming halls of the unsavory kind?

On the morning after Brian's visit, she played ball with fifteen of the team's wives after having the grounds crew move the pitching mound to the forty-three feet distance for fast-pitch softball and moving bases to sixty feet apart instead of the men's ninety.

"Looking good, ladies," she greeted them. "I love your enthusiasm, and we've already raised thirty-five thousand for the Sunshine Kids in advanced sales. So let's give everyone a good time."

"And if we can't hit the darn ball," said one gal, "at least let's look good! Where are the uniforms?"

Megan grinned. "All taken care of. Cleaned and waiting for you. Astro's colors, white with navy letters outlined in orange. Pick your numbers."

The morning flew by, and when the ladies reconvened afterwards, all they wanted was a shower. "Go," said Megan. "The locker room is yours for as long as you need it. The men are coming later. We have a night game."

"Thanks, Megan," said Amy Klein. "I really enjoy this. Except for Jeff's travel schedule, life is so good. Imagine, I'm playing at Minute Maid Park! Who would have thunk it, huh?"

Her comment about the good life made Megan pause. "You and Jeff are a strong team," she said. "His face lights up every time he mentions you."

Amy actually blushed. "Yeah, well, he can still get my juices going, and it's been five years and one child since our wedding." She peered at Megan from under her lashes. "But I hear that an ace pitcher of ours has a permanent smile on his face nowadays. Would you happen to know anything about that?"

"Whew! It's getting warm in here," said Megan, waving her hand like a fan before her face.

Amy chortled. "Oh, good one. That's all I wanted to know." She stepped closer. "Jeff says Brian's a really good guy. Those visits you send them on to the hospitals tear him apart. Actually, tear both of them apart." She pressed Megan's hand. "That says something."

"Are you sure about your facts?" asked Megan. "I've been with them several times over the years now, and I can attest that they have those kids laughing, playing catch and the place in an uproar — of a good kind. They're full of shenanigans."

"Which is exactly what those kids need," said Amy. "No matter at what cost to the men. Look a little harder, Meg. I think you'll like what you see."

She showered and returned to her office, thinking about Amy's advice and berating herself for taking advantage of Brian and Jeff. They'd never turned her down, always came through. But if Amy was right, it took a toll on them. Some of those children had gone through life-saving treatments that no one should have to experience.

Again, she hadn't looked beneath the surface. Even Amy, a lovely lady and potential friend, had to point it out. Was she so enwrapped in her own problems that she didn't pay one hundred percent attention to others who were important to her?

Whatever the future held for her and Brian, her relationship with him had opened her eyes to her own shortcomings. Judging a book by its cover was never a good idea. Read the pages, Meg!

##

Sunday afternoon's game showcased baseball at its best. Megan's entire family, except for her niece, went to see

Brian pitch. Surprisingly, despite buying extra tickets, they were all able to use the reserved box.

"In mid-August," said Megan, "lots of people are away on vacation."

"No arguments here, especially with your parking spot being available."

"Only the best for my family," she said.

"Oh, someone is a happy lady," said Nancy, "but I'm loving this privacy."

The two hours sped by, the score up and down, with Brian holding onto the lead at the beginning of the eighth, when he struck three batters out—three up, three down.

Houston scored one run in the bottom of the inning. Then Los Angeles came to bat at the top of the ninth and almost...almost brought one home. Score five-three at the end. A stadium of happy fans.

"What a game!" Craig stood and cheered along with her mom.

"Now, that's the way I like it," said Megan, rising from her seat.

"It?" asked Patrick. "How about *him?*"

Dang, if she didn't feel herself get warm. But this was her brother, so she admitted, "Yeah, him, too—even if the score were reversed."

"I liked him, Meg. Liked what I saw and heard at your house last week. And if you didn't notice, he couldn't take his eyes off you."

"Amy Klein said the same thing, and frankly, I notice all the time," she said with a grin. "C'mon, gang. Let's go. Brian will be busy recovering from the game—a massage or an ice bath or light exercise. I'll text him from the car—from all of us."

Did you hear us all cheer? Happy fans in the Ross family. Recover well and I'll probably see you tomorrow.

Not probably. Definitely. Good night.

Her brother drove everyone in his Pilot. Megan leaned back in her seat, more than happy. She couldn't remember a time when she'd felt as good about her personal life as she did now.

It seemed only an instant before Patrick pulled onto her street and headed for her house.

"Megan….," he said softly, "we've got a problem."

Megan focused ahead. "Oh, my God. This isn't a problem, it's a nightmare." Broken glass littered her driveway. The windows of her garage door were shattered. Her stomach knotted as she said goodbye to that wonderful life she'd just imagined.

"You're not going inside," said Patrick.

"Off course not. Drop everyone off at your house, and you and I will go to the police station." She studied her neighbors' homes. "It's not random, Pat," she whispered.

"There's only one person…"

"Shush."

"What's going on, Mom?" asked Josh.

"I don't know, honey. But don't worry. Uncle Pat and I are going to find out."

"I'll call a glazier to replace the windows," said Craig, "and how about collecting Samantha and all the kids having an overnight with us. It's still early. They can swim."

"Thanks, Craig. You're such a good grandpa!" Megan smiled at him. No step-grandpa in his mind, but the real thing—straight from the heart.

"It's the greatest job in the world," said Craig. "Our boys are the best. Right, kids?"

The happy chatter of the kids calmed Megan.

"This is the best day," said Josh. "A baseball game that Brian won and now swimming with the grands and everybody."

Thankfully, Josh's mind was back in his safe world of family.

An hour later, Megan and her brother stood by the car, watching two police officers return to the driveway after going through the house. One held up a plastic bag containing a baseball.

"Seems like this was the weapon. Your bedroom window's smashed too. We can probably get prints off this."

Megan nodded. "He probably didn't wear gloves. Too hot." Perspiration covered her while nausea rose in her throat. "Oh, my God. He's crazy and stupid. And I can't get my car out of the garage without flattening four tires."

"Ma'am, there's one more thing," said the officer, holding the plastic bag. "There's writing on the ball, which I'd take it as a message. It's says 50K."

Her legs shook now. She backed onto the front passenger seat and sat down.

"Do you have any idea who'd want to blackmail you?"

She nodded. "I want to take out a restraining order."

LINDA BARRETT

CHAPTER TEN

At her desk the next morning, Megan arranged for the installation of a video doorbell to replace the standard bell she had. The glass had been cleaned away the night before. She and Josh had both slept at her folks' house, and she'd driven Josh to camp as usual and told Paul to be extra vigilant.

"Routines, routines are so important," she mumbled to herself.

"Are you talking to the smartest person in the room?" asked a cheerful, familiar voice.

She tilted her head, saw Brian's wonderful, steady presence and burst into tears. He shot to her side.

"What happened? What's wrong?"

She reached toward him and stood, but only relaxed when she felt his powerful arms holding her. In fits and starts, she described the fiasco at her house the evening before. Brian kept her close the entire time, and soon she regained her composure.

"I'm okay now, Bri." But his arms tightened, and she lingered in his embrace.

"I'm so thankful you weren't home at the time, Meggie." He turned her around, leaned down and kissed her, his mouth covering hers with a hunger she recognized in herself, and she responded like a flower to the sun. Desire pulsed through her as she tasted more.

"Ahh- Meggie, sweetheart..."

Reluctantly pulling away, she tried to joke. "Our favorite game saved the day, Brian. I wasn't home."

"I'll hire another guard to stay at the house in the evening. Or, better yet, you and Josh move in with me until your ex is out of the picture."

But she shook her head. "That's what I was telling myself when you walked in. Josh needs his routine. Kids like routines, but I won't take a chance with his safety. I liked your first idea." She retrieved her purse from the bottom drawer of her desk and searched for the security company's card. Holding it up, she slipped into her chair and said, "I'm calling them now."

"You're doing everything right, Meggie. You're a lioness."

"A darn scared lioness. But at least I didn't lose it in front of Josh. I didn't cry then. I-I don't ever want to scare him."

"Come here a minute." He reached for her hands and she stood. He pulled her close again. "Crying is nothing to be ashamed of, Meg. Fear can do that. You held it all in until you saw me and felt safe." Kisses covered her temple, ear, neck. "That's such a compliment. I'm honored and glad you feel that way with me." His mouth covered hers, his kiss reassuring. "My sister, Emily, was afraid of everything. She cried all the time, and now, look at her. You're not the only one to search for some extra strength."

"Point taken, Delaney. So let's try to have a normal day—after I call Paul to see if he can work late tonight and follow me home."

"I can—"

"You have to suit up. Night game."

"I'll talk to Dave."

She held up her hand as Paul answered, nodded a few times. "Okay, good. See you later."

"You're off the hook tonight. He'll follow me home and go inside too."

"What about tomorrow? I'll set it up with Dave in case the agency can't come through on such short notice."

A big favor. She didn't like having to accept it. "You were right, Brian. It felt good playing offense last night, doing something! Like taking out that restraining order. Unfortunately, we're still mostly playing defense."

"There's a child involved, honey. It's harder. Way back, we sometimes dealt with paparazzi, but we had Luis, our driver. He was so much more, though. He knew every street in Boston and could lose a tail like no one else, and then he made sure we quickly got inside the house."

She loved hearing snippets about his childhood and learning more about him and his family. Maybe one day she'd meet them all. Maybe.

She stood up and walked to him. Putting her hands on his cheeks, she said, "Despite all the heartache and turmoil, you grew up to be a fine man, Brian Delaney. Too bad you tried to hide it from everyone."

He paused, his forehead creased and then he nodded once. "You've brought out the best in me,

Megan Ross. With you, the scars are healing. That's the truth."

Now was not the time for discussion, and years had passed, but some scars took a long time to heal. She could imagine the basis for those scars. Fear of dying young, like his parents? Fear of relationships? Fear of people leaving? And in the end, he was the one who had to leave everyone behind. No wonder he'd had a hard time adjusting to Houston.

She rose on her toes and kissed him again. "Even if you walked away from this career, I would still think you're the most wonderful man in the world."

His eyes gleamed. "Not a groupie, huh?"

"Not on your life," she said with a laugh. "But speaking of lives…"

She picked up the phone and called the security company. "Find me a clone of Paul," she told them, "and we're set."

##

Brian automatically scanned the reserved parking lot with special attention to Meg's car every time he arrived or left the stadium. Bashed windows? Flat tires? His personal radar was on alert. His schedule didn't mesh with hers on most days, and he dreaded road trips now, leaving her with one less person in her corner. Her biggest wish was for normalcy, and for the next week, he'd give that to her as much as possible.

On Tuesday morning, he, Jeff and Megan loaded his SUV with souvenirs and headed for Texas Children's Hospital. The conversation dwindled as they got closer, until the car was quiet. He wondered if little Anna was still there. He wondered how many kids would be able to join them in the lounge and how many he'd visit in their rooms. He wondered how many parents would be there. And he wondered at their strength.

He pulled into the staff parking lot and took a deep breath. "Okay gang. It's showtime." He started to sing, *Row, Row, Row Your Boat* and motioned to Jeff to join in after the second line. He glanced at Megan and pointed. Soon a silly round of the children's song was underway, and everyone's mood brightened.

Thirty minutes later, he was in the kids' lounge doing his juggling act while Jeff carried a big bag of gifts over his shoulder like Santa Claus. And while Brian juggled, he pulled out from memory some of his corny jokes, with Jeff acting as his straight man. Anything for a laugh.

"Hey Jeff, what did the traffic light say to the car?"

"I don't know, Brian. What did the traffic light say to the car?

"Don't look. I'm about to change!"

He saw Megan's eyes roll, but some of the children laughed, and he kept juggling. "Hey kids, the lady didn't like that one. Should we try another one?"

"Yes! Yes!" A chorus answered him

"Hey, Megan. Why was the little strawberry crying?"

"I don't know, Brian. Why was the little strawberry crying?"

"His mom was in a jam!"

The kids giggled, and he smiled to himself. Megan hadn't looked too happy about participating, but she'd gone along with it, and that's what mattered. Too bad that in real life, Josh's mom was in a jam.

"Bri-an, Bri-an," A sweet, familiar, little girl voice called.

He caught the three balls, then pivoted around to see seven-year-old Anna walking into the lounge with her mom and waving to him.

"There's my girl!" He kneeled in front of her, glanced at her mom for permission and lifted her into his arms.

"Oh, man, you're getting so fat and heavy, I can hardly pick you up!"

Her giggles meant everything. "Remember last time, after my treatment, when we had our special date? And you made me feel better? Then I went home for a long time. But I had to come back for a treatment. I'm so glad you're here today!"

"I'm glad too, baby."

"Only two more times," she added.

He glanced at her mother, who nodded.

"You are a beautiful, warrior princess, Anna." He put her down gently, kissed her on her cheek. "Ready for some baseball stuff?"

He looked for Megan, who was in charge of the tote bags, and saw tears starting to well. He trotted right over. "Hey, baby, buck up. You'll cry later."

"It's not that, I mean, it is but…" She shook her head. "Little Anna was your date! That day in Dave's office when we met for this crazy assignment. You said you had to leave because you had a date with 'a very special lady.' And it was Anna."

He remembered that day clearly, and liked to think he'd kept the others off-balance during that little surprise interview. Four against one. Some odds. "Yeah…well, I don't lie, but I don't always go into details. And certainly not then. But now, everything's cool."

With plastic bats and balls, he and Jeff put on a slapstick baseball show for ten minutes, then talked up the Houston Astros, gave out children's T-shirts, caps, coloring books and magazines.

Then he took down names for the Astros Kid List. "Jeff and I are going to play Thursday's game in your honor," he announced. "You can watch on television and look for your names on the big screens in the park—the Jumbotrons."

As they were leaving the lounge, he glanced at Anna and her mom. "Let's sign a real ball for them, Jeff. They need a special gift."

When they were back at the nurses' station, he took a deep breath. "Okay, folks, now for the hardest part." He checked with the charge nurse. "Who's expecting a visit today?"

"Come on, Champ. I'll personally escort you. They're excited, actually."

"Can't let 'em down. You coming, Jeff?"

"We're a team, aren't we?" His friend looked beat, unnerved, but rallied.

Brian pointed at Megan, whose complexion rivaled white linen. "You stay here." She nodded without a fight, very unlike her, and Brian figured her own worries about Josh's safety had magnified in the hospital.

"The thing about boys," he said a half-hour later, as they walked to the parking lot, "is that they really want to talk baseball. And that comes naturally to us."

"Yep. It does," said Jeff, "and for a little while, they're not thinking about anything else."

"I wonder," said Megan, "why I never noticed this empathetic side of you before, even though we've been to Texas Children's a couple of times."

"Maybe you saw only what you expected to see," Brian began slowly, "or maybe I didn't let you in."

##

Security systems were installed at her home that same night, and Megan allowed herself to relax a bit. She'd arranged not only for a video doorbell, but a home security camera above her garage. Another several hundred dollars earmarked from her bonus money, which she hadn't received yet. But as she'd said to her mom and Craig when they came over to inspect, "What price peace of mind? And I can now check any activity from my cell phone before I even turn onto my street."

"I can't believe it's come to this," said Kathy. "Lee's been missing in action for over seven years! He was a-a lightweight, let's say, and I knew he'd started gambling, and had that woman, but I never thought he was truly…evil."

Whoosh. "That's a strong word, Mom, especially from you, who always sees the glass as half-full, even after all this time. A natural optimist with a sweet nature, I guess." She motioned them inside. "C'mon, both of you, and stay for supper. I'll toss a big green salad with some ham and cheese. Wine wouldn't hurt either. And… I think I have a garlic bread in the freezer. Perfect."

She liked having her family around. Sharing a cool meal on a hot summer's evening hit the spot, and Josh got some alone-time with his grandparents.

"Mom, can I go ride bikes with Tommy and Peter? They're outside."

Of course, he wanted his usual freedom, but… "Maybe later. You've been running around all day. How about…"

"How about another chess game with your old gramps?" asked Craig. "Let's see how much you remember. I've been wanting to coach both you and Trevor together. You're almost good enough to challenge him."

"I am? Okay! I'll tell my friends, then get the set." Josh ran off.

Megan approached her stepdad. "Thanks, Craig. I'm not comfortable right now with him riding through the neighborhood where I can't see him."

"I don't blame you, honey. Hopefully, Lee will disappear again, or better yet, find himself behind bars. And soon."

Her fervent wish. The police were working on the case, but she couldn't simply trust it to happen. He'd seemed pretty desperate for money when he'd accosted her outside the restaurant over three weeks ago, and the home invasion reinforced his need. Too bad she didn't have a fairy godmother to make wishes come true.

The high-pitched, excited voices in the locker room on Saturday morning brought a smile to Megan's face, reviving memories of her own college softball career. She'd played every position at some point, but wound up taking over second base during her final two years. She'd worked hard and played hard, which turned out to be a winning combination later on. Her playing experience had come in handy at her job.

"Good morning, ladies! I love the energy, excitement and enthusiasm. A great way to start."

"The only thing missing, Megan, is the talent!"

The women cracked up, but one called out, "The other team might be worse."

Megan laughed, too, and realized once again that this game was not at all the same as her college games, where her team truly played to win.

"Are you ready to have some fun and raise a lot of money?" she asked.

"Are you kidding?" replied Amy. "My whole extended family bought tickets, and I convinced every friend I have to show up—with their kids."

"Great," said Megan. "I recruited celebrity umpires— sports announcers and the weather gal from one of our Houston radio stations. They'll work the crowd, too. Our job is to entertain and—" she beseeched, "at least try to win. Play hard, if you can. You need to give the ticketholders something to root for."

"The ticketholders? What about my husband?" said Julia Watson. "Travis will never let me hear the end of it if I drop the ball *every* time I handle it."

"Like he's perfect?"

An amused Julia replied, "No one's perfect, but I have to admit, he practices all the time. In fact, too much. That tendinitis flared again last week."

"Hm," said Amy. "We've had, what, two practices?" She turned to Megan. "Do you really think that's enough?"

Megan took her time answering. "Frankly, no. I love working with each of you ladies, but… are you familiar with the expression, 'herding cats'?" Her gaze traveled from woman to woman. "We had a tough time arranging the practices we did have with everyone schedules so different from one another's."

Silence met those words.

"She's right," said Amy, "but I have an idea." She turned toward the others, and asked, "How do you feel about forming a real team that plays all year long? I, for one, love playing this game instead of just watching all the time."

Go, Amy! Megan surveyed the women, saw their enthusiasm build as, one by one, the idea settled into their minds. Pleased with herself that she'd been part of instilling a liking for the game, she stood quietly and let their plans unfold. A consensus of yes had an excited Amy twirling toward her.

"And Megan, can you play and be the coach, too?"

They had no idea about the situations in her personal life, about her fear for her son's safety as well as her own, about her growing relationship with Brian, about how her job was so varied she wasn't always behind a desk. Making a commitment would be hard to fulfill. But...

"Yes. I'd love to. I can't resist the prospect of having some real down-time." And not worrying about anything but softball for a couple of hours each practice. "If you organize it, I'll be there. In the meantime, we have a game to play!"

By one o'clock, her entire family was seated along the first base line. Brian was also in the stands behind home plate, not suited up but in his regular cargo shorts. The men didn't play until seven. She had a job to do, but could feel his eyes on her as she ran up and down the base lines, giving advice to her players and again in the dugout, when he and too many of the men started standing close by, trying to offer tips.

"They're getting a taste of the 'watching' part," Julia said with a giggle. "They'd rather be on the field, playing it for us."

"Ignore them," said Megan. "This is your game." She wiped her face with a towel. "And you're doing great. Okay, batter up."

She walked outside the dugout and motioned the guys away. "You're distracting them. Move!"

Brian put his hands up and backed off. "Love the ponytail, coach. Looking like eighteen." He laughed, and to Megan's amazement, joined her family, most of whom he hadn't met before. Shaking her head, she admitted it was typical Brian. He'd just cut through a lot of red tape, her red tape. He'd wanted to meet her peeps, and now he had.

It was probably time for that anyway. He'd been so much a part of her life all summer, she didn't want to keep him a secret anymore.

Her team's eventual win was no secret either. Her Astro wives squeezed it out by one run. They shook hands with the Dallas team, waved to the crowd and ran the bases as their male counterparts cheered and joined the ladies back in the dugout.

Megan wasn't ready to call it a day. Whether the game had worked as a pressure-cooker release or her adrenaline needed somewhere to go, her energy level remained high, and she started running the bases again. Before she blinked twice, she had a partner.

"I've got a glove. Wanna catch?"

Oh, yes. Yes, she did. She tossed him a softball and ran to the infield. Easy at first. Throw and catch. Throw. Catch. Then harder. Further. Brian jogged toward home as she went toward second, still throwing, making her run for it. She sensed him judging her, accelerating their play, but just enough. Safely. She felt his pace, remained in synch with him. He said nothing, simply communicated with a look, a nod, a gesture. She read his sign language and reacted automatically. Such a high!

Soon, the stadium faded away and the people along with it. Except for one person. Brian Delaney. She wanted to continue this catch with him forever.

With Brian, forever? She almost dropped the ball.

Brian waved her in, and only when reality returned did she hear the whistles, applause and shouts from her team, family and others.

"Take a bow, Coach. You deserve it." Brian was clapping for her, too.

"Thanks so much, Bri. I felt wonderful out there, so good just enjoying the moment without stressing about anything." She kissed him on the cheek. And sparked a chorus of calls and whistles.

"Oops. I think it's time for a shower," she said. "Then I'll head out with Josh."

"I'm pretty sure he's going with your brother, so no rush." Brian gestured toward the family group.

She entered the dugout and found her purse. A quick text to Patrick confirmed Josh's whereabouts. *Thx. Home soon. C u at the pool.*

"I'm sorry, but I can't stay for tonight's game," she said to Brian. "That kid and I need some time together."

Brian nodded. "I totally get it. Have a great time with him. But text me when you leave, and I'll walk you to your car."

LINDA BARRETT

CHAPTER ELEVEN

Brian held Megan's hand as they strolled to the parking lot. Her fingers intertwined with his as naturally as if they'd been resting that way forever.

Forever. His heart skipped a beat. He glanced at her again just as she looked at him—and smiled. Now his heart ricocheted in a rhythm he'd never experienced. Fast, slow, up, down. All over the place.

He leaned closer and kissed her. And like a match to kindle, she responded. On a sidewalk outside Minute Maid Park, where the world could have passed by, where, in fact, some people were walking by. And he didn't give a hoot.

He drew her closer, kissed her again. Loved feeling her lean on him. Loved everything about her. "Meggie," he whispered, "I want to hold you forever."

He heard her sigh against him and listened. "I know you do. I feel it, too. Even on that ball field when we were playing catch…I wanted it to last all day and night. And now I want to stay right here." Her blue eyes shone, but a shadow lingered. "But I can't…until…after…we know what…

"Sweetheart, I'm not afraid of him. Don't worry."

"I want to start clean, Brian. With clear skies and no baggage hanging like an albatross around our necks. Especially mine."

"You have a beautiful neck," he said, and kissed her again, wondering how he could assure her of her safety. Of Josh's safety. "C'mon. Let's get you going."

They walked into the lot and up the first deck, past the row of cars on the right. Megan's reserved spot was toward the back.

"I'm sure we'll be watching tonight," she said, as she slipped behind the wheel.

"Hey, I'll be watching too, from the dugout!" He leaned into the open window and kissed her again. "Drive carefully."

He jogged slowly back down toward the entrance, thinking about other ways to ensure Josh's safety without scaring him. Megan had done a great job by having Danny and Paul as part of his day camp. But if the situation didn't resolve soon, they'd have to extend his protection to school and other activities. A crappy way for a kid to live.

He paused when he got to the entrance and looked back. He didn't see her car coming down the ramp toward him. Strange. Engine trouble? A flat tire? Nah, he would have noticed a flat.

So he'd get extra exercise today. He started jogging back toward her spot and immediately saw the dark sedan blocking her vehicle.

124

Her car wouldn't move when she put it into reverse. It shimmied, sort of off balance. She sighed and unlocked her seat belt, opened her door and stepped out into the garage again.

"Like a lamb to slaughter. Such easy pickings." The familiar voice sounded nasal and unhinged. She snapped to attention but didn't have time to think. He grabbed her by the front of her shirt and slammed her against the closed car door. He stank from sweat and stale beer.

She squirmed and twisted, then opened her mouth to scream.

His hand clamped across it. "The money. I told you I need the money."

She kicked and shook her head, tried to bite him.

Crash! Her body jerked up straight at the sound of breaking glass. Lee spun around. Megan pulled her head back. Her car's rear window shattered. She turned around and saw Lee reach into his pocket. *Oh my God. No, no, oh no.*

He pulled a gun just as a baseball slammed into his head and he crumpled like a rag doll.

"The dumb bastard should have asked me for the money," said Brian, running to Megan, his cell phone in hand.

Megan shook all over, wanted to vomit. Her arms encircled her stomach, and she just tried to breathe. Sounds came out of her mouth that weren't words. As if from a distance, she heard Brian talking to Security about an ambulance, about police, and then he was holding her, leading her away. Soothing her, as if she were an infant.

"Shh. Shh. Everything's cool, Meggie. He's out of our lives forever now."

"…a gun…he had a gun…oh, my God…don't tell Josh…" Her broken thoughts, scattered at first, started coming together. "Gone forever? Oh, Brian, did you kill him?"

"I probably should have, but the bastard's leg just twitched."

She almost laughed, but… "Where's the gun, Brian? Where's the gun? Does he have it?"

"Nope. I left it where it landed," he replied immediately. "Underneath his own car. Let the police do what they have to do. But I'm going to move you a tad to my right, so my left hand's free. I still have another ball in my pocket. Just in case."

And then she did laugh. But once she started, she couldn't stop. Words emerged between gusts. "Pitching and juggling. You're always prepared. I knew you were a Boy Scout."

"Meggie, please. You're scaring me, and I can't wrap both my arms around you right this second."

"I'm good. I'm good," she said, while trying to catch her breath. "Megan Ross doesn't fall apart like some wussy little girl. Not her style." She must really be in a bad way to talk about herself in the third person.

"Megan Ross is entitled to do whatever she wants today. Anyone would be entitled. Besides, my Megan is a lioness. You know that. And it's just the way I like her."

She raised her head and stared at him. "Really? Not too bossy? Too impatient? Too hard-nosed?"

"Not too anything. Just perfect."

Her chuckles this time were tinged with delight. "Now I know you're the right guy for me."

"Sweetheart, I am the only guy for you. Have I told you that I…

Two police cars, lights and sirens roaring, came up the ramp. An ambulance right behind them.

…love you?"

Three little words. The most important three words in the world. "No, you haven't. And your timing is terrible."

"To be continued. Just hold that thought until after the docs look you over."

##

He didn't suit up that night, and he didn't want to fly to Chicago with the team on Monday. But he had no choice about that. He'd be on the mound Tuesday afternoon. But for now, he was going with Megan.

"Ready to go home?" he asked.

"More than ready. I-I want to hold Josh in my arms and never let him go."

"Of course, you do. I get it," he replied as they entered his SUV. "But you don't have to be afraid anymore."

Her car had been towed, the police had come and taken Lee away, but not before they ticked off the charges against the perp — now they could call him a perp. Having an unlicensed gun, assault with a deadly weapon, and breaking the conditions of a restraining order, for starters. Then there was his connection to an illegal gambling syndicate. They were very interested in that, too.

Brian drove down the now-cleared ramp as evening settled over the city, and a quietude settled within his car. He glanced to his right. Megan seemed more at peace, but not totally relaxed.

"Want to talk about it some more?" he asked. "Get it all out of your system? Mine, too, for that matter."

"Sort of," she said. "I have to tell you something important that involves Josh. And now seems the right time."

Which meant nothing could be more important. "I'm listening." He was glad the traffic seemed unusually light.

He heard her clear her throat. "Josh does not know Lee is his father. I threw the man out when our son was six months old, and he couldn't leave fast enough. He had a girlfriend, too." She paused. "I actually found them...God, I was so stupid."

"You weren't stupid. Just young. Everyone makes mistakes, Meggie. Don't beat yourself up. Besides, look at you now. You're terrific, and Josh is super-great. A win-win."

"You're very sweet, Brian. Thanks."

"No thanks needed. It's true."

"There's more to the story," she continued. "Legally, Josh is all mine, with my last name, too. Just in case I haven't mentioned it, I wanted you to know that I went to court. There are no loose ends. That man has no claims."

"I get it, Meg. I think it was a smart move, actually one I'm very familiar with." Memories swirled like the contents of a distant photo album. "After the accident, Lisa fought for us in court. She was almost twenty-three. My mom's sisters wanted to take us in—we loved them—but they would have split us up."

He glanced over. "I haven't thought about this in years, Meg. But Lisa was a tiger—just like you. She dressed us in our Sunday clothes, and we sat in the courtroom, good as gold—well, mostly good as gold. Mike was there, too, but he and Lisa weren't married yet. She was appointed our guardian." He felt Megan staring at him, listening closely.

"That's an amazing story," Megan said quietly. "Your sister sounds incredible, and I do see some parallels with me, but still...wow. Four kids."

"I like incredible women!" said Brian, stopping at a light and grinning at her.

She squeezed his thigh. "All I want is a peaceful life."

He felt the heat where she touched him and covered her hand with his. "But I do have a particular question," he said, noting the hoarseness in his voice.

"Anything," she said. "I don't want secrets between us."

He didn't either. Not with Megan. "Has Josh ever asked you about his dad? It would be a natural question." The light changed, and he kept his eyes on the road, giving her a bit of privacy to gather her thoughts.

"Yeah, he actually did ask, a few years ago, when he was old enough to make connections."

She became silent after that, and he glanced at her again. She was gnawing at her lip. He knew she had more to say, but wasn't sure about it.

"Go on," he encouraged.

"I told him," she finally began, "that his father and I had divorced, and that later on, he'd died."

The steering wheel jerked in his hands. "Died? That's big, Megan."

"It wasn't an easy decision, "she replied. "The man didn't want a child hanging around him. He didn't even fight me for custody. Can you imagine, he didn't want his own child! As Josh got older, he'd probably start asking questions. What should I have said? Your dad's alive but doesn't care a fig about you? Should I have let my son feel the sting of such a huge rejection?"

"No, of course not." When he thought of the wonderful dad he'd had, the kind of dad every kid deserved, the word rejection wasn't even on the vocabulary list.

"My way was cleaner," Megan said. "Now Josh doesn't ask where his father is, or why we divorced. I've learned, Bri, that sometimes with a child, you tell them what they need to know—at the time they need to know it. And that's all."

Silence permeated the air while he considered her words. "Little by little, hmm? I guess it's better for their hearts and souls."

Her smile could have lit the night. "Exactly. Later on…much later on…if something comes up, hopefully, he'll be better able to handle it."

He reached for her hand and squeezed it gently. "Lisa and Mike had no roadmap for parenthood either. They did the best they could under the circumstances. And, in the end, I guess we turned out okay."

She began to sob quietly.

"Oh, Meggie, what? What did I say?"

"You-you turned out wonderfully well. I'm so relieved that you understand, so thankful you get it. I never realized how hard it could be to share my most personal thoughts and decisions with someone not in my family."

"I love you, Megan. You can tell me anything."

##

Two cars sat in her driveway while lights blazed from the windows of the house. "Looks like the gang's all here."

"They want to make sure you're okay," said Brian. "In case you didn't notice, we did not have an ordinary day. So..uh..tell me, Meg. Are you okay now?"

A good question, but she had no definitive answer. "Ask me tomorrow. Let me see if I have nightmares."

"I won't have to ask. I'm staying over tonight, and no arguments. I'll be a gentleman and take the sofa. Not gonna ruin a good thing with Josh in the house."

"Got it all figured out?" He looked so cute, with just a tiny trace of anxiety. "How do you know I'll be that patient?"

His laughter resonated joy. "I'll be ready for you anytime."

They entered the house and were surrounded by family, questions and lots of hugs. Craig and Patrick wasted no time before shaking Brian's hand and clapping him on the shoulder. Kathy couldn't stop hugging Megan, her hands stroking her daughter's face, examining her everywhere.

"Everything's fine, Mom. I promise.

From the center of the hub came one high and loud voice. "Would somebody please tell me what's going on?"

Megan swirled around to her son. Trevor and Samantha stood on either side of him, looking confused as well. Her mind raced as she thought about how to explain. "I will, Josh, but first let's all go into the living room. This hallway's too small." Buying time was also a good thing.

The three children stuck together as the family followed her suggestion. She sensed Brian close to her, as she walked directly to the kids. She glanced at each of them, but her eyes remained on Josh.

"So, the important thing to know is that the excitement, shall we say, all ended well. Everyone's fine. But we did have a little incident after the softball game." The entire room was quiet as everyone focused on her. "Someone flattened my tire and then grabbed my shirt and tried to rob me in the garage at work." She held up her purse. "Stupid guy didn't even know how much I had."

"Mom, you never have any money! The guy was really stupid."

She ignored the chuckles and leaned down to hug her boy before standing again. "Brian showed up at exactly the right time and beaned him with a baseball. The cops came almost immediately and took the guy away." She brushed her palms together in a dismissal gesture. "All done." And no need to mention the gun in front of the kids.

Josh turned to Brian, then leaned against Megan. "I'm glad you were there."

Brian squatted to be eye-level with her son. "I was very happy, too. Your mom is a special lady to me, and I'll be hanging around here more in the future."

"You mean after the Chicago trip?"

Megan felt a grin begin. "I can't believe this kid! He must have memorized the team schedule."

Trevor pivoted toward his younger cousin. "Don't you get it, Josh? Brian likes your mom. He really, really likes her." His exasperated tone had Megan laughing again.

"She's a princess!" exclaimed Samantha. "And he's her prince!" Samantha seemed to get it in a heartbeat.

Megan watched her son's jaw drop open as the proverbial coin dropped in his mind. He looked from Brian to her, then back to Brian.

"You mean like-like what Sammy said?"

"Your cousin's a smart girl, except for one thing. I'm not a prince. I'm just a guy who loves your mom. And I hope that's okay with you, Josh, because it's really important to me that you're okay with it."

Megan's breath hitched. The entire room seemed to hang with bated breath, waiting for Josh's response. But Josh still had a question mark written on his face.

"Does he mean, Mom, that he loves you...like...forever? Like Auntie Nancy and Uncle Patrick?"

And right there, her son cut through to the heart of the matter. She felt her eyes fill. "Why don't you ask Brian?"

But he didn't have to. "I mean forever," said Brian, standing and walking over to Megan. He held out a hand to Josh. "I have faith we can figure this out, Josh. What about you?"

Josh looked from Patrick to Craig before approaching Brian. "I have an uncle and a grandpa already," he said. "But...but...I've never had a dad." He clasped the man's hand.

Brian leaned down and dropped a kiss on Josh's head. "Then that makes us even. I've never had a son before, either."

"But like you said, we can figure it out, right?"

"Absolutely."

Megan held her breath as Josh's glance traveled to her. Then her son nodded and said, "Okay. Let's do it."

She reached for both of them and pulled them close. "You guys are amazing. I love you."

A round of applause followed. Megan raised her head in shock. "Oh, my goodness. I forgot ya'll were in the room!"

##

Hugs and words of congratulations had followed. Not to mention phone calls from Boston. News concerning a prominent MLB pitcher aired quickly. And Brian's experience in the parking garage had qualified as news. It took more than hour before Megan, Brian and Josh were alone.

But it took no time for Josh to start yawning. "You have lots of family, Brian. Am I going to have more aunts and uncles?"

"You bet. And four more cousins. You'll love Bobby. He's eleven and loves sports, just like you and Trevor. But he's a football kid."

"Well, considering his dad is Mike Brennan..." said Josh in between yawns.

"Come on, tiger. Into bed with you," said Megan. They'd reached the point where being overtired could ruin the whole evening.

Josh started to walk away, then turned. "Do you want me to show you where my bedroom is?"

"Lead the way," said Brian.

"You two go," said Megan. "I'm going to just relax right here." She lowered herself to the sofa and stretched out. When they were out of sight, she called Paul with the update, thanking him profusely. His assignment was over, and she'd let the agency know.

After disconnecting, she glanced more closely at her cell and saw an enormous number of texts. Flipping through the first ones quickly, she then started to slow down. "Oh, wow, oh, wow."

"Hey, sweets. Josh is already in dreamland. What's going on here?"

She held out her phone. "All the wives on my softball team reached out. If I need anything, want anything, even a cup of tea and their company. Who knew I had so many friends? I've always loved my career, but this—this support is so much more than that. Amy Klein offered me her car until mine's fixed."

"Jeff and Amy are a great couple, but if you drive me in tomorrow, you can use the SUV for the week. In fact, Meggie, I was thinking..."

"Hmm?" Unexpectedly, she was feeling drowsy herself and her eyelids began to close.

"Let's repair it and trade your Civic in for the larger model sedan. We've had bad luck with that car. It's a jinx."

Her eyes opened wide again. "Trade it in? There's nothing wrong with the motor."

"I didn't say anything about the motor."

She started to laugh. "You're sweet, Bri, but get over it." Reaching for his hand, she said, "No superstition involved here. No jinxes. Not random. So we're not wasting money trading a car that's only four years old."

He leaned back and she heard, "Deja vu all over again."

"What?"

"Never mind. You need some time to adjust." He studied her. "Meg — I have a lot of money. Savings. Investments. In fact, Jen manages a bunch of my accounts. Trust me, we can afford a new car."

She'd spoken with his sister on the phone earlier. Sounded like a lovely person, concerned about Megan and the aftermath of the attack. "You've got a lot of sisters I have to navigate through. I don't want them to think I'm with you for the wrong reasons."

"Sweetie, all they need to see is the smile on my face, and they'll know the truth." He leaned over and maneuvered himself next to her in the narrow space.

His mouth covered hers gently, nibbling, his tongue stroking her lips, tasting her and then...a kiss.

That's all it took—one lovely kiss to set her ablaze. Her arms wrapped around his neck, and she captured him with a hunger that was new to her. More than simple sex, more than anything she'd known in the past. Desire for the right one. With this man, everything was right. She'd been ready to know him for a seemingly long time.

"Brian...?" She peeked up at him, and he paused. "This sofa is not big enough."

In one motion, he stood, held her aloft in his powerful arms and headed down the hall. "I was hoping you'd come to that conclusion," he whispered.

She blew gently into his ear, and he almost dropped her. "I believe you," she said softly. "But just so you know…it's been a very long time—for me."

He placed her gently on her bed where she'd slept alone since Josh was a baby, and kneeled down next to her.

"You're the coach, my love. I'll handle the protection, but you call all the shots."

And she did. The kissing, the touching, the exploring. Until there was no he and she. But simply them. And afterward, she couldn't stop tears from streaming as she lay on her side with her arm across his chest. "I'm so happy," she said.

"I've heard of happy tears," he said, "but I've never seen them. Are those them?"

She nodded vigorously.

"My love, you're tearing my heart open." She felt him stroking the back of her neck, her earlobe. "But it's a great feeling. I love you, Meggie. I didn't know it then, but when I walked into your office that first day, it was the luckiest day of my life."

"So, we're back to luck again?" These baseball fantasies and superstitions would never end. This time, however, she was amused. "Let's say that it was a lucky day for us both."

"You are the perfect one for me. When I get back from Chicago, let's go shopping. I want a ring on that finger."

"Afraid I'll disappear?" She chuckled, then sat up and caressed his cheek. "There's no chance of that. I love you, too, Brian Delaney. We're finally on the same team now, each of us pulling our own weight but sharing the responsibilities. Does that sound right to you?"

"Sounds exactly right. Perfect. Everything's perfect. Especially you." And with those words, he fell deeply asleep, as though his mind was finally at ease.

She bestowed a kiss on his cheek. "Perfection is impossible," she whispered, "but I'm certainly not going to argue."

Kissing him again, she rolled on her side and felt his arm come across her. She snuggled closer and allowed herself to drift off, too. Maybe Brian was right. Lying next to him felt kind of perfect.

LINDA BARRETT

CHAPTER TWELVE

A week later, Brian was back in town, and Megan took a vacation week from work, her usual routine at the end of August. She and Josh were in Brian's kitchen on Monday morning— a luxury because the Astros had the complete day off. Josh watched in awe as Brian built his breakfast.

"Carbs and protein are the way to go," he explained while creating a massive egg-white omelet with toasted bagel and peanut butter on the side. "Enough for everybody," he said. "Josh, could you grab some orange juice from the fridge?"

Megan listened and watched them interact while she set the table. So natural. A good foundation.

"So what's your plan for today after you drop me off at the clubhouse?" asked Brian.

"Camp's over, and school starts this Thursday," Megan explained. "Josh and I have some shopping to do." She grinned at her son. "That boy does grow every year."

Josh glanced at Brian. "I hate the shopping part, but I like the growing part."

"That sounds exactly right," Brian said. "I felt the same way as you when I was a kid. Eventually, sick of our complaints—can't forget about Andy—my sister just shopped without us and bought the same stuff every year, only bigger."

Josh's eye lit up. "Hey, Mom. That's a great idea. You could—" He paused and turned back to Brian. "How come your mom didn't buy you clothes? Only your sister?"

Brian glanced at her, a question in his eyes, and she nodded. "Make it as simple as you can," she said.

"My mom and dad weren't around," he began quietly. "They were already in heaven. So my big sister, Lisa, and her husband, Mike took over. And that's why Lisa bought the school clothes every year."

In the following silence, Megan watched her son process the information. A wrinkled nose, creased brow, and then, wide eyes as he understood. With no hesitation, he walked over to Brian and leaned against him. "I never had a dad either, but I'm glad you had your sister. And you know what? Now you, me and Mom have each other, sort of like a family. And nobody will be alone anymore."

Megan listened, blown away by Josh's words. *Where did this child come from?*

"How about a hug, tiger?" Brian's voice sounded raspy. He grabbed her son around and drew him to his chest. "You are a fantastic boy, Josh, to figure that out. You are absolutely right. Except for one little thing."

"What?"

"Not 'sort of like' a family, but definitely a real family. Mom, Dad and son. How's that sound?"

Josh sought her out. She nodded, and her son smiled at her before turning back to Brian. "Sounds perfect."

##

An hour later, Brian stepped into the clubhouse and headed to the bullpen, looking for Rick. The breakfast time with Meg and Josh had put him in an upbeat mood and, *Oh, What a Beautiful Morning* quietly reverberated in his mind.

Rick was coaching Travis Watson, who was scheduled to pitch the next night in their first game against New York. The man looked good to Brian. He hoped his tendinitis was a thing of the past.

"Hey, Delaney," said the pitching coach. "Come back in an hour."

"Videos, Rick. I want to see the Yankee lineup. And...I also want videos of me. The good, the bad and the ugly. I want to put a plan together."

Rick stopped mid-motion. "Now you're talkin' my language, Brian. Every pitcher needs a plan—a routine for the days in between games—especially you."

Especially him? "I guess I don't have one yet, is that it?"

Travis started to crack a grin while Rick gave Brian one hundred percent attention. "You're not lazy, but you've been all over the map. And I told myself and you, if I remember correctly, that I could only get you so far."

Had Megan done the rest?

Even if that were true, the self-absorbed jerk that he was had never given Rick the curtesy of working seriously with him. "Well, I'm making some changes," said Brian. He'd work harder, clinch his career, and provide Megan with anything she wanted—a big diamond, a bigger house with a pool of their own. As for Josh—the sky was the limit

"Sure he's making changes," exclaimed Travis, "because he's a man in love!"

Brian grinned and pivoted toward his pal. "From what I can tell, I'm not alone in that."

A thousand-watt smile crossed Travis's face. "I've got some advice to get you started on the right foot, although with Megan in our business, you may not need it."

"What kind of advice?"

"The money kind," replied Travis. "This career we have pays well. You know that. But it can be a bit overwhelming for our gals, especially in the beginning. Julie grew up working class, similar to Megan. No silver spoons. And Megan's got a kid, and proud to be raising him. I made the mistake of throwing a load of money at Julie in the beginning. Buy this, buy that. Big house. Fancy neighborhood. She hated the whole idea. She's still uncomfortable with too much. Too much at once can be an issue. So, go slowly. Put it in the bank."

He thought about Megan's car and her reaction to buying a new one. He thought about Lisa and Mike's arguments when he was a kid. "I hear you, and thanks. Now I know that reaction's not unusual."

Scratch the big house idea. In fact, he didn't have to come up with all the solutions. That's what a partnership was all about.

For the first time in his life, he'd met a woman who made his heart dance. For the first time, he had his own family to care for. He was planting roots in a new place, and it wasn't bad at all. Now his thoughts focused on tomorrow rather than yesterday.

Studying videos, however, did not require a partner. His work in the bullpen had his name only on it.

Win, lose or draw, he'd make an honest effort and do his best. Show Megan she could count on him.

She was late to the game Thursday afternoon. Josh's first day of school ended at noon, only a half-day. By the time they ate a quick lunch and got on the road, they arrived at the end of the third inning and went directly to her regular box.

Only a few co-workers were there. For most employees, it was a regular workday. Brian was on the mound.

"He's having a very good day," said Carla softly, just as Brian struck out the Yankee's second batter of the inning. "So far, eight up and eight down. Have a seat."

She plopped into her chair and watched Brian strike out Number 9.

"Three perfect innings," she said in amazement. "That's unreal, even if the luck stops now. How much talent does my guy actually have?"

"Sometimes talent burns out quickly, and sometimes it takes a while to blossom," said Carla, who'd been around the game for many years. "My advice is to enjoy it."

"Easy for you to say," said Megan. "My tummy feels like a bunch of jumping beans took up residence."

Her cell rang at the bottom of the fourth perfect inning. Dave Evans.

"Are you in the stadium?"

"Yup. With my son."

"Brian's having a good game."

"Yup."

"Get to the dugout when it's over. The press will be there no matter how it ends. Our boy is making noise."

"Of course."

She disconnected and looked around at the very familiar setting. She knew Minute Maid Park inside out, from top to bottom. She knew the game inside out as well. But suddenly, she knew nothing. Nothing about what went on inside Brian's mind when it came to his career. It was all so matter-of-fact in the past, almost superficial. Do this, do that. Practice, massage, eat right. Follow the rules. But where were the rules about what he was doing right now? How would she ever understand what went on inside a talented man like Brian Delaney?

She was just a working mom. He'd become larger than life. Maybe she'd been living in dreamland all summer. Maybe their relationship was simply an interlude until he found his footing. Now her stomach really hurt.

Dammit! Annoyed with herself, she focused on the game for another two excruciating innings identical to the previous ones. Her tension mounted along with the fans', and she couldn't sit still for another minute. Time seemed to slow and race at once. Brian had not allowed even one hit. She left Josh with Carla while she visited the dugout.

It was filled with silent men. Brian wasn't there, but she saw a man's shadow in the runway, pacing. Brian's shadow. She slipped away—no jinxing— and walked toward the dugout fence. Jeff gave her a thumbs-up but said nothing. The scoreboard showed 1-0, Astros. And the fans seemed quiet.

Breaking into that hushed atmosphere came the announcer's voice. "That's three outs and the Astros take to the field at the top of the seventh with Delaney back on the mound. It's been eighteen up and eighteen down so far in this beautiful ballpark on this beautiful August afternoon. Houston fans are loyal here and happy with their club...."

He's babbling. Megan shook her head, slapped her ears. The voice was babbling inconsequential nothings. The crowd was quiet. The men weren't talking, either in the dugout or as they moved onto the field. She came to a halt, absorbing the moment. Then watched Brian at work.

Focus on one player at a time. Keep them guessing. He knew every man's weakness and played to it. Slider, curve, changeup. Surprise them. His new little family was in the park, and he wanted to win for them.

Three outs! It happened so fast, as though he were in a stupor. Now the Astros were at bat. He jogged to the dugout and sat in his usual spot. Funny how quiet it was. He looked at the scoreboard. "Good, we're ahead so far."

"Yeah. We are," said Jeff. "And you're up, Delaney."

It seemed noisier when he approached the batter's box, but he shrugged. He wasn't an elite hitter, not like Andy. He aimed to be respectable. This time he hit a grounder toward third, but was out at first.

No one said anything when he returned to the dugout and dropped on the bench. He glanced at the scoreboard. "Too bad about the grounder."

"It's a good game, Brian," said Jeff softly.

Then everyone was quiet again, looking at the floor, the field, everywhere but at Brian. He shrugged and thought about the next batter he'd face.

"So is Joe Morales up next inning?" he asked Dave.

"Yup. They didn't change the order."

Brian nodded. "He bats lefty and low ball. I'll surprise him."

"Sounds good."

"Jeff? Sound good to you?"

"Definitely," said the catcher.

He retired Morales, he retired Brown, and he retired Clayburg. In the bottom of the eighth, the team scored another run.

And then there was one inning to go.

##

Was Brian aware that he was in the midst of pitching a perfect game? Megan could barely believe her eyes. *A perfect game.* A special no-hitter with no walks allowed, no one on base due to errors, and no balls hitting the batter. It was rare, so rare that hard-core baseball fans knew the names and dates of the twenty-three pitchers who had ever achieved it in all of baseball's history. Over a hundred years!

She took a deep breath. Then exhaled. Pacing behind the dugout, she could barely make herself watch the play. But little by little, she came forward and stood, eyes glued to the mound.

Batter 25—gone. Batter 26—gone. One more to go. She closed her eyes, crossed her fingers and sent up a little prayer. Absolute silence reigned in the park. Then she watched Brian throw six times before he sent Batter 27 off the field to his own dugout.

The stadium exploded. His teammates rushed the mound, fans screamed Brian's name and the announcers were screaming praise and their own spin, probably making up for all the quiet and nonsense they'd been restricting themselves to during the game.

A pair of thin arms encircled her waist. Josh, with Carla behind him.

"Couldn't hold him back," she apologized, her eyes sparkling. "What a game! What a game!"

"It certainly was! Carla — if you have the numbers in your cell phone, can you call the Red Sox organization and let his brother know? Brian would like that."

The woman went to work. "Got it." She was quiet for a moment, delivered her message, and then added, "and would you mind contacting Mike Brennan — I'm sure you have the Riders' back office number somewhere. And I'm sure Mike would want to know. Thanks. Thanks a lot. Yeah, it's very noisy here. Put on your television!"

"Thanks, Carla," said Megan. "Brian's close with his family." She gazed at the field where the party was still going on. The stadium stayed packed. Seemed the fans wanted to be part of every last moment. "Let's broadcast the interviews on the jumbo screens."

She called Dave with the idea, and he did the rest. But she remained near the dugout. Just waiting. Watching the celebration with his teammates on the field.

Finally, finally he was waving and running toward her. A second later, she was in his arms, being twirled in circles. Being kissed and hugged. Being loved.

"I didn't know what was happening," he said, "until about the eighth inning. All I wanted to do was win the game and improve our standings."

"You are full of surprises," she said, "even surprising yourself."

He reached for Josh and lifted him. "A good day, huh?"

"I love you, Brian."

"Same here, son."

Any thoughts she'd had about simply being part of an interlude for his career disappeared. Love was written all over his face. Toward Josh, toward her.

Ten minutes later, they convened in the press box. Megan began to organize the event, but Brian pulled her back.

"Today, I'll take over." He grabbed a microphone and faced the media. "You'll get to ask questions in a minute, but first I have something to say." He took a breath and began. "This game is dedicated to all the kids out there—every girl and boy who's dreamed of being a professional athlete, dancer, musician, writer or whatever is in your heart.

"I dreamed of playing baseball all my life, but as I got older, I discovered that it wasn't easy. In fact, it was darn hard. I learned that what used to be a game turned out to be work—lots and lots of work. Many times, I thought that maybe I wasn't good enough. And I almost stopped trying. After all, if you don't try, you can't fail. But I really loved the game and stuck with it. So, kids, never give up. Keep playing your piano, throwing that football, pitching that baseball, writing that story, studying for medical school—do whatever you love. Just don't give up your dreams."

He was making it hard for her to do her job. Beautiful words spoken with sincerity and warmth. The crowd cheered again.

With the microphone at his side, he said, "I love you, Meggie. I never want to let you down." His lips touched hers, warm, loving.

"You got it right, Brian," she said. "Trying is all that matters. Not the winning or losing. Just doing your best."

"And I'll never stop." He turned toward the press. "Okay, ask away."

Josh spoke up first. "Wait. You forgot the best part of the story."

"What's that, Josh?"

"When you try hard, you get a great ending. You, Mom and me. And it's not a game. It's real."

"Amen."

##

HOUSTON CHRONICLE — SPORTS—Feb. 15th.

DELANEY TIES the KNOT

Hometown Astros' favorite pitcher, Brian Delaney, and Megan Ross said "I do" to each other yesterday in the elegant lobby of Union Station, the grand entrance to Minute Maid Park, and the perfect venue for these two loyal Astros fans.

Escorting the groom down the aisle were his sister, Lisa Delaney-Brennan, and brother-in-law Mike Brennan, the Boston Rider's elite quarterback.

Ms. Ross, wearing a classic Vera Wang gown, was escorted by her mother and stepfather, Kathryn and Craig Fanning of Houston.

Best man for his brother was Andrew Delaney, power hitter for the Boston Red Sox organization.

Groomsmen honors were held by Doug Collins, Broadway playwright and brother-in-law to Brian, and Jeff Klein, Astros catcher, and Travis Watson, Astros pitcher.

Matrons of honor were Nancy Ross, the bride's sister-in-law, as well as Jennifer Delaney-Collins, the groom's sister.

Maid of honor was Emily Delaney, the groom's sister and renowned classical violinist.

Not to be forgotten was ring bearer, Joshua Ross, the bride's son, and his cousin, flower girl, Samantha Ross.

While a deeply personal event, this Valentine's Day wedding showcased a rare combination of attendees whose names are familiar to everyone in the world of sports, music and contemporary drama. In fact, the groom confessed that mid-February to mid-March was the only off-season time for the brothers simultaneously.

An extraordinary family, and all of H-Town wishes the best of luck to Megan and Brian as they carve out new beginnings on their perfect day.

The End

HELLO FROM LINDA

Dear Reader—

Thank you so much for choosing to read *Safe at Home,* the second story in my brand-new series, *No Ordinary Family.* If you enjoyed watching Megan and Brian find their way to happiness, then I think you'll also enjoy the next story where Brian's younger sister, Emily, is about to discover true love.

In the third book of the series, *Heartstrings,* Emily Delaney is a successful world-traveled solo violinist, but is stuck at home after suffering injury to her hand and shoulder. Orthopedist Scott Miller can fix her up if she follows the rules of recovery. Love has no rules, however, which is something the good doctor has forgotten. An excerpt from this story follows this letter.

You'll also find a second excerpt here which shines a light on why the Delaney siblings are *No Ordinary Family.* In *The Broken Circle*—the book that started it all—you'll be introduced to the Delaneys in their growing up years where the spotlight is on Lisa and Mike.

If you enjoyed reading *Safe at Home,* please help others find it so they can discover Linda Barrett books, too. Here's what you can do:

- Write an honest review and post it on Amazon, Barnes & Noble, iBooks, Kobo or any of your favorite book sites. Short is good!
- Keep up with me at my website at: www.linda-barrett.com to find out about upcoming books.
- Sign up for my newsletter on my website.
- Tell your friends! Word of mouth is still the best way to share news about a book you've enjoyed.

I'm sincerely grateful for your help in getting the word out about *Safe at Home* and my other novels, which are listed below and available both electronically and in print.

Thank you very much for being a Linda Barrett fan. I truly appreciate you!

Best,
Linda

.

EXCERPT FROM
HEARTSTRINGS
(NO ORDINARY FAMILY SERIES BOOK THREE)

He couldn't believe his good luck. Dr. Scott Miller felt
as giddy as a kid with a double scoop ice-cream cone as
he entered Boston Symphony Hall on a Saturday night in
mid-October. He'd gotten a last-minute invite from his
friend, Andy Delaney, whose younger sister was the
guest soloist that evening. His older sister couldn't make
the concert—thus, the available seat at the sold-out
event.

"I'm looking forward to this," he said to Andy.
"When I saw her play at Tanglewood two years ago, she
held that audience in the palm of her hand. Including
me!"

"She does know how to use that bow," said Andy, grinning. "Surprises me all the time. I guess…to the family...to me, anyway, she's just Emily, my kid sister."

"Who happens to be a violin virtuoso." Scott shook his head. "I play the oboe in the Doctors' Orchestra here in town. The group is great—almost professional—and we raise a lot of money for charity. But your sister's in a class by herself."

"Emily doesn't practice medicine and do surgery on the side," said Andy. "Cut yourself some slack! Geez, why do I hang out with such overachievers?"

Scott laughed heartily at his friend's remark. A power hitter for the Red Sox, Andy and the baseball team could all be called overachievers, training and training —sometimes overdoing it, too. They were all part of Scott's orthopedic practice at Mass General, where he was part of a sports medical team that included an array of therapists, trainers, nutritionists, psychologists and physicians.

They found their seats in the front-orchestra section, and Scott couldn't rein in his high spirits.

"I had a pretty crappy week," he said, "but music is my reward for dealing with patients who don't listen! Who seem to think all I need to do is wave a magic wand and all their pain will disappear."

"Wouldn't that be great? A quick fix. So, what do you tell them?" asked Andy.

"I tell them I'm a physician, not a magician. And if they want to heal, they'd better listen closely and follow up." He sighed. "It's the same speech I give to you and the guys, but sometimes…" Sometimes, his heart broke—like when he worked with the elderly and their joint issues, such as crippling arthritis. For these wonderful seniors, he wished for that magic wand, but settled for therapeutics and microsurgery to ease their pain and improve their lives.

Scott opened the program notes just as the house lights started to dim. Leaning back in his seat, he exhaled and relaxed. It didn't matter what pieces were showcased. Tonight, he'd replace his patients and responsibilities with the joy of listening to wonderful music—and finally meeting Andy's sister.

Twenty minutes later, after a short orchestral piece, Scott kept his eyes locked on the petite brunette who walked across the stage with the violin in her hand. She wore a long, sleeveless blue dress—plain, but perfect on her—and low-heeled shoes. He noticed details. A good physician had to observe, had to ask questions, and listen to what was said and what remained unsaid. Those skills came to him naturally now.

The audience welcomed her warmly, this home-town girl from a family well-known in the city. She turned to the conductor, nodded and raised her violin, then waited for the opening notes from the orchestra. In a heartbeat, she joined and led them through the long first movement of the *Sibelius Violin Concerto*. She played with the emotional mix of foreboding and delicate sweetness the piece required, before continuing through the second and then the third, which ended with a happy, upbeat feeling.

The woman was amazing. Thirty minutes, non-stop. Never faltered through all three movements, almost dominating the orchestra. The wild applause, the bravos, including his own, echoed through the hall until she left the stage.

The house lights came on for intermission, but he remained seated, just absorbing the experience.

"That's strange," said Andy, his brow wrinkling. He looked at Scott, stood and headed toward the exit. "She always plays my mom's theme song after each performance. I think it's in her contracts."

Scott rose. "Keep walking," he said. "I remember that, too. *Amazing Grace.* She played it at Tanglewood. I'm right behind you."

##

He followed Andy out and around and through some hallways, pausing while he identified himself to ushers and security. Finally, they knocked on a dressing room door.

"Em, it's Andy and a friend. Are you decent?"

"Come on in."

She sat bent forward on a cushioned chair, cradling her left arm on her lap, her left hand limp, her eyes shiny when she looked up.

"Andy! So glad you're here. I'm in a lot of pain. I can't drive myself home."

Her brother walked closer to her and knelt to her eye level. "What happened? In there"—he pointed back to the concert hall area—"you played magnificently."

Scott could have kicked himself. Some doctor. He'd noticed nothing wrong when she played. But now he noticed a lot and couldn't restrain himself from speaking. "I'm afraid what happened, Andy, is that your sister abused almost every part of her body that she needs for playing. It's not only her hand. I'll bet it's her neck and shoulder, too. She's in trouble."

Her chin lifted, her eyes snapping fire at him. "And who are you, besides Andy's friend, who thinks he knows it all?" Her sharp words couldn't hide the painful gasps Scott heard as she spoke.

Her brother stood and looked Scott square in the eye. "She may not want to hear it, but I do. First impression, Doc?"

"She's an unbelievable violinist with a will of iron. That's my first impression. As to the rest…" Here's where he'd be the bearer of bad news, but not yet...."I'd need to do an examination in the office."

He turned toward Emily. "How did you get through this performance? Cortisone shots?"

She stood, turning her head to face him, and winced. "They're not illegal."

"True enough." He extended his hand. "My name's Scott Miller. I'm with Mass General's Orthopedics Department. Andy can fill you in."

She looked at his hand but waited. "Orthopedics? Do you want to test my right hand? There's just a touch of discomfort there too." She extended her arm, and he took her hand in his, but didn't shake it. Instead, he gently pressed her palm and the inside of her wrist with his thumb. Saw her wince.

"And there's the answer to what happened to *Amazing Grace* this evening," he said.

"I'll play it later at home," said Emily, "It's once a day for me."

Shaking his head, he said, "No. No, you won't. You shouldn't. From what I can see, your entire body needs to rest. Try singing instead. There doesn't seem to be anything wrong with your voice."

He grinned, slapped Andy on the shoulder and stepped toward the door. "I'll find my own way home. "And you," he said to Emily, "take care of yourself. The risk of ignoring injury is very high." He turned to leave.

"We'll need another driver," said Andy. "Can you take Emily's car, Scott?"

"Of course," he replied, reversing steps. "Should have thought of it myself."

"It can stay overnight in the lot," said Emily. "I don't need you—umm—I don't want to put you out."

Or accept a favor. "You've already given me some beautiful music," he said. "I'm happy to help."

She seemed to hold her breath before making the effort to stand. Taking a step toward him, she tipped her head back to meet his eyes. "Do you really want to help, Dr. Miller?"

He braced himself for what was coming. She'd want a miracle.

"Then get me through the new year," she said. "A couple of months. I have concerts scheduled—luckily in the States—Florida, New York, Philly, the West Coast. Whatever the cost, it's more than worth it."

He glanced at her brother, who just shrugged and nodded his head. "She's in the middle of the music season, and if she breaks her contracts…?" Andy emitted a low whistle in an off key. "That would be tough on her finances and her reputation."

So now he had to convince Andy too?

"Let me put it this way," he said, eyeing them both. "The longer you ignore treating the symptoms *properly,* the higher the chances of ruining your career—*permanently.* So, Ms. Delaney—Emily— you decide the cost."

This was so not the way he'd envisioned the evening. He'd pictured them all going out for a late dinner or a drink or even coffee, and celebrating her performance. Having a good time. What a dreamer!

"What-what do you mean by *permanently?"* she asked, her voice quivering.

He glanced at Andy. "Tell her how many players are no longer on the starting roster due to injury. And I don't mean a broken arm. I mean due to repetitive motion injuries. Especially pitchers."

Andy's brow furrowed, and he sighed. "He's got a point, Em. Brian takes care of his arm like it's a baby. The Astros have a whole medical team, just like we do, and our happy-go-lucky brother actually follows instructions. After all," he said, grinning, "he's a married man now, with responsibilities."

That comment drew a quick return smile from the woman. But then she closed her eyes, as if gathering her thoughts or her courage—he couldn't decipher which. Slowly, her lids reopened, and she stared at him for thirty seconds, up and down, but mostly at his face.

"Are you the best orthopedist in Boston?" she asked quietly.

"Boston is filled with excellent physicians," he said, hoping to avoid hubris—or idiocy—by protesting too much. "I always advise new patients to get a second opinion. In your case, Emily," he continued, "I should probably be the second opinion. Feel free to search out whomever…

"No!" interrupted Andy. He turned to his sister, "He's the one. I don't care if you don't like his direct approach, he's the one you want."

"Figures," she murmured. "So that's settled." She looked up at Scott. "And you should know I'm stronger than I look."

"Stubborn is what she means," said Andy.

A tiny smile began at the corners of her mouth. Sweet.

"Sing with me, Andrew," she said, her smile growing. "Let's sing it now—together. As always, for Mom and Dad." She glanced at Scott. "Grace and Robert." Slowly, her soprano voice filled the room, each beginning note as beautiful as the notes of her violin. *Amazing Grace, how sweet the sound…*

Her brother's tenor joined her in a duet with an ease that bespoke a lifetime of making music together. Without quite realizing how it happened, Scott found himself creating a trio. And it sounded remarkably good. Two choruses of the hymn, and Emily made a cutting motion with her arm.

"Maybe there's hope for you," she said to Scott, a quick smile appearing and then suddenly gone. "I'm praying that there's hope for me. Because without being able to make music and soar with my beautiful partner over there," she said, pointing at her violin case, "I have nothing."

She'd packed quite a punch with her last remark. Of course, she was wrong, but her dressing room after the concert wasn't the place to argue. Scott sat behind the wheel of Andy's car, following his friend to Emily's apartment in the Back Bay area of town. Great neighborhood for a young professional like her...or him. But he was happy with his spot closer to the hospital on Longfellow Place, where medical personnel almost filled the building.

He watched Andy pull into what was probably Emily's or a neighbor's reserved spot and double-parked, prepared to wait. But his friend surprised him.

"Go on in with her while I try to find a meter. You need to get to know her a little. And vice versa. I think she trusts you now, so keep going easy on the keys, if you know what I mean."

He understood exactly. A softer approach. He exited the car quickly, ready to put his and Emily's initial introduction to rights, and walked to her vehicle. The passenger door was still closed. He tapped on the window and opened the door. In the glow of the streetlight, he saw big, beautiful brown eyes fringed with thick long lashes peep up at him. Dark chocolate eyes.

"I know you're in pain," he said quietly, "so you tell me how to help."

To his complete astonishment, tears started to fall, which made his heart almost stop. "What? What did I say? Your brother's going to kill me!"

"Sorry, sorry," she replied, rubbing her wrist across her eyes. "It's just that it's so hard to hide this, and now I'm not alone."

His breath hitched. A powerful statement, both revealing and true, but even though he was with her now, she'd probably hate him later as they moved toward diagnosis and treatments.

He swung the door wider while she pivoted herself around so that her legs dangled outside the car. She wiggled closer to the edge, preparing to stand.

"Your back?"

"No. It's my neck and shoulder, and of course, my hands. I'm a mess."

He offered his arm, and she steadied herself as she stood. "Well, that's an achievement."

"It's amazing how you played the concert tonight," he said.

"That's how it works. I was in another world."

"No pain in that world?" he asked dubiously.

She was quiet for a moment, until she eventually said, "Think of it as an out-of-body experience. I know it sounds weird, but that's the way it works—for me. Or should I say, worked. Past tense, because now it's more intense."

"I'm sorry about that. I suppose eventually you can't outrun your fears and have to face them."

A quick glare. "Are you speaking from experience, Scott?"

The sweet lady had a sharp tongue. "I've learned from the experience of my patients. Everyone has fears. And I don't live in a bubble, either. But have I crossed the line again?" he asked, gazing ahead. "I still volunteer as the second opinion, regardless of your brother." He pointed down the street. "And here comes Andy."

Emily turned toward her brother. "Can you get my joyful noise out of the back seat? I'm not leaving her."

Andy grabbed the violin, and they entered Emily's building, a well-maintained Victorian brownstone, the type often found in the Back Bay area.

She led them to her first-floor apartment and managed to unlock the door. A small entryway led to a large living room, which seemed to serve as her personal practice studio. Sheet music, music stands, a sound system for listening, and an upright piano as well as a sofa and table filled the space.

But Scott's attention was on the woman as he took out his cell phone. "I'm checking my calendar for openings," he said, "to get you into the office. Are you sure about this?"

"The sooner, the better," she replied.

He stared at the week ahead, trying to manipulate appointments. If his schedule was any fuller, he'd have no time to sleep. "Morning surgeries are set in stone," he murmured, shaking his head. "But if…okay. Maybe." He looked at her. "The soonest I could see you for an initial workup is Tuesday at three. I have to be somewhere else at four—but very nearby. So if that works for you, I'll put you in. To save time, you can fill out all the paperwork I'll send you ahead of the appointment and present it at the reception desk."

"Anything works for me," she said. "If you have a card, please write the date and time down and put it on the table. Holding a pen is a bit painful." She extended her right hand. "My bowing hand. It's really not too bad, and it's not swollen. As you said, I'll rest it."

He took out his wallet and did as she asked, then entered her phone number and email address into his cell. "In case something changes."

"Oh, I'll be there." She looked toward her brother. "Thanks, Andy. I owe you one."

"Just answer some questions and you'll be out of my debt."

"Not now." She glanced at Scott. "My brothers have a tendency to be over-protective. Both of them."

"We love you, Em. And that's not going to change." Andy started pacing. "So why were you alone tonight? Where's Mrs. Merri? I thought she accompanied you on concert nights. Where's your manager? Why did you drive yourself?"

She stepped back. "Whoa! Slow down." Her foot tapped several times. "Mrs. Merri has a heavy cold, and I told her to stay home." She glanced at Scott. "Mrs. M. was my very first violin teacher, and before that, my third-grade music teacher. Without her..." she shook her head, then addressed Andy again.

"And Larry's gone from my life." Suddenly, her eyes blazed hot fire, something Scott hadn't seen before. "That two-faced thief. Two weeks ago, at dinner with the London concert manager, we talked about future concert dates and costs, including my fees. The London guy kept saying that I was expensive but worth every penny of my fifty-thousand-dollar contract."

Her voice trailed off, her brow creased, and those lovely eyes became shadowed. "I was confused. My contract was for thirty, a fair and standard amount. And that's how I caught on to how Larry was fleecing me." She glanced from one man to the other and said, "I was so upset that I made excuses and left the table. He was gone from the hotel the next morning. Ran off before I could confront him."

She paused and looked at Andy again. "I guess Jen didn't tell you?"

"Not really. Just said that she was researching something for you." He glanced at Scott. "Jen's my financial whiz sister, with Fidelity, but it's Lisa, the lawyer, who should be helping get a warrant for the man's arrest!"

Emily stood still and Scott heard her inhaled breath. "She is, bro. She is. I guess no one is exempt from the reality of business, not even a concert musician." She walked to the sofa, held her head perfectly straight as she lowered herself, and gestured for them to sit anywhere they wanted.

"To answer your last question," Emily continued, "I drove myself tonight because I'm stupid! I should have taken an Uber."

"Or called me!" said her brother.

She glanced at the violin. "My future with Joy is what's upsetting me most. She's on loan until the end of December—only two more months! Normally, I'd be able to renew the three-year arrangement, but if I can't play, I'll have to return her."

Her voice broke, and Scott hoped she wouldn't start crying again. She'd been fearless about playing, fearless in her anger at the manager, fearless about getting herself to Symphony Hall. But now, her fear was at a breaking point. That was what a blend of worry and love could do. He'd seen it often with his patients when they first came to see him. When they left with a plan of action for determining a diagnosis and possible treatments, they'd become calmer. Knowledge was power— trite but true.

"What do you mean, on loan?" asked Andrew, regaining Scott's attention.

"Your sister is playing on either a Stradivari, a Guarneri del Gesu, an Amati or another outstanding Italian prize going back to the early 1700's," Scott said. "None of us could afford her — not even a slugger for the Red Sox—at least, not yet."

"He's right," said Emily. "I call her Joy. She's a remarkable Strad, an amazing girl who's meant to be heard, and not purchased by a collector and placed behind glass. If I have to give her up…"

"Stop borrowing trouble," said Andy. "Six months from now, you'll be on stage again, and this - this" —he gestured widely—"crazy interlude of legal and medical messes will be in your rearview mirror."

"I'd drink to that, if I had some wine," said Emily. "Instead, I'll take two pain pills and call my sisters in the morning."

"What are you—" began Scott.

"Over the counter, Doc," Emily interrupted. "No worries. I'm desperate, but not stupid—except for driving tonight." She grinned up at him, and for the first time that evening, he felt they were communicating as two ordinary people—man and woman.

He acknowledged her grin with one of his own and saw her eyes widen.

"You should do that more often, Scott," she said softly.

"Right back at you, Ms. Emily Delaney."

She looked more than pretty when she blushed.

The thought blindsided him. Pulled him up short. He'd trained himself not to notice those things, to avoid women he might want to know better. In his life, relationships led to trouble. He'd almost flunked out of college because of one. Had it been love? Sex? Freedom? Probably a combination. Where would he be now if he hadn't come to his senses? He'd come so close to disappointing his folks, such hard-working people and so proud of him.

The breakup had been awkward. He'd wished her well and soothed her ego. Assured her she'd been competing with his scholarships, not another woman. But he'd been careful ever since. From college to

165

medical school to residency to being on staff, to building his reputation in orthopedics and then sports medicine—there were always goals. Further involvement with women had no strings attached—a mutually understood condition—involving none of his co-workers. Fortunately, making music with the Doctors' Orchestra provided an emotional outlet.

He'd figured out what worked for him back then. And after all his effort, the devotion to his career wasn't going to change. He wondered, however, if there was now room in his life for a lovely woman with chocolatey brown eyes. Or if she'd turn his life upside down. He wondered if he wanted to find out.

EXCERPT FROM
THE BROKEN CIRCLE
(NO ORDINARY FAMILY SERIES BOOK FIVE)

January 1995
Boston

A knock at her grad school apartment door pulled Lisa
Delaney away from Commonwealth of Massachusetts
vs. Torcelli Construction. Eyes burning, she rubbed her
lids while, from her iPod, she heard Bryan Adams insist
that everything he did, he did for her. Old song. Easy
words. If the man really wanted to impress, he could
take her contracts exam in the morning.

She pushed away from her desk, covered in law
books and case briefs, and rose from her chair,
stretching, bending and groaning. Her knees creaked like
an arthritic old lady's. Shaking her head, she emitted a

long sigh and promised herself a gym visit the next day—after the exam.

A second knock echoed, this time more impatiently

"I'm coming. Hang on." Nimble again, she rushed across the room and opened the door.

Her eyes widened, her stomach began to roil as she looked at two uniformed state troopers, snow melting on their jackets, cop faces in place. Her thoughts raced with possibilities. Classmates? Mike? Oh, please, not Mike.

"Are you Lisa Delaney?"

She stared at bad news and froze. All of her. Nothing worked. Not her mind, tongue, or breath. Perhaps her heart had stopped, too. One man coughed. The other repeated the question.

"I-I'm Lisa."

"Are your parents' names Robert and Grace Delaney?"

Oh, God, yes! Her heart raced at Mach speed, but she couldn't feel her legs at all. "What happened?"

"May we come in, Ms. Delaney?" Taller cop.

She nodded and pulled the door wider, but the knob slipped through her sweaty hands and she lost her balance.

"You might want to sit down."

As though moving underwater, she struggled into the closest chair.

"I'm afraid there's been an accident on the turnpike," began the quiet-till-now officer. "A fatal accident."

"Not…not my…my parents?" She barely got the words out before the officers' sympathetic silence answered her question.

"But that's impossible! I just spoke to my dad…"

"When was that, ma'am?"

When? When? "I think…maybe…last…last night…." Her voice drifted. Daddy had been checking up on his eldest, his numero uno child, joking with her about an apple a day. Staying healthy. A convenient excuse to call. To keep in touch with the one who'd left home. She'd understood his M.O. a month after arriving at school. Sweet, loving man. A man with a phone.

"Wh-what...?" Her throat closed.

The cops seemed to understand her intent. "The official investigation is ongoing, but according to preliminary reports, the other driver lost control of his vehicle and did a one-eighty."

"Drunk? But...but it's the middle of the week." As if that fact could change things.

"The driver's blood alcohol was normal."

"Then what...? The road...?"

"Icy conditions contributed. The temperature drops at night, and your folks were approaching at just the wrong moment. There were no survivors. I'm very sorry."

She nodded. *No survivors? Mom and Dad?* She wanted to cover her ears.

The other officer looked at his notes and said, "The Woodhaven police are with your brothers and sisters."

Oh, God, the kids... She had to get back to Woodhaven!

Standing quickly, she was hit by a wave of nausea and fell back into her chair. She doubled over, hand on her stomach. The phone rang, startling her further. She stared at the instrument, half-buried by textbooks, reached forward, and slowly lifted the receiver. "Hello?" she whispered.

"Lisa! Lisa! The police are here. Mom and Dad were in an accident. You have to come home! Now! I'm scared."

Jennifer. Her social butterfly teenage sister whose life revolved around boyfriends, best friends, and having fun. Except, not tonight. In the background, she heard the cacophony of younger voices crying and talking at the same time. She heard little Emily's high-pitched wail. "When is Lisa coming?"

"Hang on, Jen." She took a breath and looked at the officers. "There are four of them. Emily's only seven. My twin brothers are nine. Jen's sixteen. I've got to get there—a hundred miles—and I don't own a car." She couldn't afford one and didn't need one in a city with mass transit.

The troopers nodded, and she spoke into the phone again.

"I'll be there soon, Jen. As soon as I can. Maybe William and Irene can stay with you meanwhile." Her fiancé's parents lived across the street.

"They're not home. They went to Miami to see Mike play. Didn't you watch the game yesterday?"

"Of course I watched, but I didn't know his folks flew down." Mike had subbed for the starting quarterback and played an entire quarter. It was only his first year, but now the Riders were in the play-offs.

"So, Jen, you need to be in charge now until I get there. You and the kids sit tight and wait for me." She glanced toward the window, where falling snow was reflected by the light of the streetlamps.

"It might take a little while," she added. "It's a big trip, and the roads are bad…" What was she saying? Her parents had just been killed on those roads. "Jen, honey, let me talk to one of the officers there."

Her hand shook as she gave the receiver to the state cop. "Ask if they told the kids the truth."

In seconds, he shook his head. "Not yet. They're getting a social worker in on it."

She raised her eyes to his. "Please tell them not to do or say anything until I get there. Okay?"

Perspiration trickled from every pore. She shivered and sweated until finally her stomach lurched. Running into the bathroom, she vomited until nothing remained. Then she brushed her teeth, packed her suitcase to the brim, and snapped it shut. The sound focused her, and she inhaled a deep breath. *Be strong, be strong...*

One of the troopers held the door open. Her gaze skimmed the small apartment. She'd been happy there and ecstatic at being accepted into the program. She glanced at her textbooks before locking on to her college graduation photo. Her parents stood on either side of her, their smiles wide.

"Oh-h... One second." Her own future was now uncertain. Dropping her suitcase, she darted to the wall, took down the picture, and tucked it under her arm. Their dreams and her dreams might have to wait awhile.

#

Michael Brennan needed three days to get home to Woodhaven and to Lisa. It seemed like three years.

He tossed his luggage in his parents' front hall, turned around, and headed directly across the street. The Delaneys lived in a two-story wood-framed house with a front porch similar to his and to all the other homes on Hawthorne Street. He'd grown up there, but Lisa and her family had moved in over four years ago in June, right after her high school graduation. He'd graduated from a neighboring high school that same year. Their paths hadn't crossed until the evening his mother baked a cake and insisted their family welcome the new neighbors. Moaning and groaning, he'd given in, and the Brennans had gone to visit the Delaneys.

When Lisa opened the door and walked outside, he'd almost tripped up the front steps. One glance and he couldn't speak. His brain froze, too, as if a lightning bolt had slammed him head to toe. Big violet eyes, long, dark wavy hair, and a killer smile. A friendly smile. *Who wouldn't have fallen in love with her?* But he'd been the lucky one, the lucky guy who'd relished every single day since Lisa Delaney had first appeared at that front door.

Now her sidewalk needed shoveling. The streets had been plowed since the storm a few days ago, the walkways, too, but snow had fallen again yesterday, and surfaces had turned icy. He flexed his shoulders and entered the house. He'd take care of the snow after he wrapped his arms around her...if he could find her.

The Delaney house was packed. He recognized Lisa's aunts and uncles from out of -town, and all the neighbors, of course. Lisa's closest friends, Sandy and Gail, were there, too. Either they'd stayed all day or had just come from work. He waved and searched for his mom.

"Where's Lisa?"

"I'm glad you're here, Michael," she said, giving him a quick kiss, "but don't expect too much from Lisa. She's overwhelmed as...as we all are." Irene Brennan gazed up at the ceiling, indicating the second floor. "She's got the kids with her. The funeral's tomorrow, and she wants time alone with them."

"Alone doesn't include me."

He took the stairs two at a time, sensing the glances, the sympathy of the visitors as he made his way up. He appreciated their support, but they didn't have to worry. Surely, he could handle whatever he found. Surely, he and Lisa could handle it together.

He paused in the hallway at the top of the stairs. Each of the four bedroom doors stood ajar, but he could hear nothing. He started to push the first door open when, from the end of the corridor, he heard Lisa singing quietly, "Too-ra Loo-ra Loo-ra, Too-ra loo-ra lie..."

Was she trying to put the kids to sleep at five o'clock in the afternoon? He slowed his pace and walked the last few steps before knocking softly and entering the master bedroom. Lisa sat on her parents' bed, leaning against the headboard, the twins dozing on either side of her, little Emily sleeping on her lap. Jennifer lay across the foot of the bed, also sound asleep. He took it all in and understood that day and night had no meaning to them.

"Lisa..." A whispered prayer.

Her red-rimmed eyes brightened, her arms opened, and he was there. Kissing her and gently shifting one little brother lower on the mattress. She began to cry, her tears mingling with his as he rained kisses, and his tension melted simply by holding her in his arms. Tears flowed as he continued to embrace her and grieve while remembering Grace and Robert Delaney.

They'd been wonderful neighbors, wonderful parents, and good friends with his folks. The Delaneys had worked so hard to finally become "owners" instead of "renters," and celebrated their move to Hawthorne Street each time they'd made a mortgage payment. Lisa had told him how her dad would brandish the check and twirl Grace around the kitchen every single month. With their growing family, it had taken them fifteen years to afford their own home.

"How long can you stay?" Lisa whispered.

"He can't," mumbled nine-year-old Andy, rousing slightly. "He has to go to the conference championship game. And maybe to the Super Bowl."

"But not yet," Mike said, rubbing the boy's head with affection, but focusing his gaze on Lisa. "I'll be here for the funeral tomorrow. You won't be alone. Then I'll be back in a week. One short week." Which might feel like an eternity to Lisa.

"I'm glad, but-but everything has changed," she said, pulling a tissue from the nearby box and blotting her face. "We need to rethink our plans."

"The basics haven't changed," he replied quickly. "I love you, Lisa Delaney. And don't you forget it."

Her eyes shone. She pressed his hand, her fingers narrow and delicate around his broader ones. "I love you, too, but-but...." She sighed and glanced at the assorted children. "I'm not sure what's going to happen next," she said quietly.

"I am," he said. "I'm going to kiss you again."

And he did. When she kissed him back, when she lingered and leaned against him, he almost collapsed with relief. She was *the one* for him. No matter what. Her needs, the kids' needs....

"We'll sort it out when the time comes," he said. "I'll support you in every way I can." The logistics would no doubt be complicated, but he had faith that he and Lisa could do anything as long as they did it together.

She offered a wan smile. "I know you'll do your best, but you have commitments to the team. You're so talented! We all know you're being groomed as a starting quarterback, maybe even next year. So I think, for both our sakes, I need to handle this-this family situation by myself."

No, she didn't, but her brave effort tore a corner of his heart. "I think you're right about my place in the team," he said slowly, "but that's in our favor. The money's good." He'd worked hard with his coaches, and his natural talents had been recognized. His dream career loomed just over the horizon.

"I must be weird," said Lisa. "I never think about your salary. Even your first year minimum is like make-believe Monopoly money to me. It doesn't matter. I'm just so...so proud of you."

Men cry. Even big football players. But once that afternoon was enough. His throat ached as he swallowed to stem more tears. Lisa needed him to be strong.

"Have I ever told you about my conversation with your dad at the end of the summer you moved to Hawthorne Street?" he asked. "It was right before I went off to Ohio State on my scholarship."

"All Daddy told me was that you were too big for your britches, but he was laughing."

A surge of love and a wave of sadness—both raced through Mike. The words sounded exactly like something Rob Delaney would say. And the laughter—well, laughter was the norm in Lisa's family. Her dad loved to tell a good story and could imitate the comedy greats and their jokes. Rob had been a natural "on stage," and no one had a bigger heart.

"Before I left for college," Mike continued, "I told him I was going to marry you someday."

"You've got to be kidding! We were only eighteen. We'd just met that very summer." For a moment, her expression lightened. She tipped her head back, and her eyes met his. "And what did he say?"

"He said that I'd better treat you like gold—always. And I promised I would."

"O-o-h...." Despair once again etched her face. "Our lives... everything..."—she waved her arm— "has changed. I can't-I *won't* hold you to any promise."

"You have no vote." He kissed her again, vowing to keep that promise. Loving Lisa was the easy part. Building a solid future together...well, that goal might be more difficult to reach now. Lisa was in no condition to make any decisions. Their next steps would be decided by him.

His gaze rested on each of the youngsters, one at a time. Four sweet, innocent children. Without warning, his heart started to race, and his palms became covered in sweat. Fear. Like Lisa, he was almost twenty-three, and deep down, he was scared, too. He had no experience with kids, not even a younger brother or

175

sister. But he wouldn't give himself away, wouldn't let Lisa know. A quarterback led with confidence on the field. Now he had to do the same at home.

LINDA BARRETT BOOKS

NOVELS—ROMANCE

No Ordinary Family Series
Unforgettable (Bk. 1)

Safe at Home (Bk. 2)

Heartstrings (Bk. 3)

His Greatest Catch (Bk. 4)

The Broken Circle (Bk. 5)

Starting Over Series

True-Blue Texan (Bk 1)

A Man of Honor (Bk. 2)

Love, Money and Amanda Shaw (Bk.3)

The Inn at Oak Creek (Bk.4)

Flying Solo Series

Summer at the Lake (Bk. 1)

Houseful of Strangers (Bk. 2)

Quarterback Daddy (Bk. 3)

The Apple Orchard (Bk. 4)

Pilgrim Cove Series

The House on the Beach (Bk. 1)

No Ordinary Summer (Bk. 2)

Reluctant Housemates (Bk. 3)

The Daughter He Never Knew (Bk. 4)

Sea View House Series

Her Long Walk Home (Bk. 1)

Her Picture-Perfect Family (Bk. 2)

Her Second-Chance Hero (Bk. 3)

NOVELS—WOMEN'S FICTION

The Broken Circle

The Soldier and the Rose

Family Interrupted

For Better or Worse – A boxed set of all three WF novels at a discounted price

SHORT NOVELLA

Man of the House

MEMOIR

HOPEFULLY EVER AFTER: Breast Cancer, Life and Me (true story about surviving breast cancer twice)

Printed in Great Britain
by Amazon

49117664R00106